Triplets

Becky's Terrible Term

HOLLY WEBB

■SCHOLASTIC

Scholastic Children's Books
An imprint of Scholastic Ltd
Euston House, 24 Eversholt Street
London, NW1 1DB, UK
Registered office: Westfield Road, Southam, Warwickshire, CV47 0RA
SCHOLASTIC and associated logos are trademarks and/or registered trademarks of
Scholastic Inc.

First published in the UK by Scholastic Ltd, 2004
This edition published by Scholastic Ltd, 2014

Text copyright © Holly Webb, 2004

The right of Holly Webb to be identified as the author
of this work has been asserted by her.

ISBN 978 1407 14474 0

British Library Cataloguing-in-Publication Data.
A CIP catalogue record for this book is available from the British Library.

Printed and bound by CPI Group (UK) Ltd, Croydon, CR0 4YY
Papers used by Scholastic Children's Books are made from wood grown in
sustainable forests.

This is a work of fiction. All characters, places, incidents and dialogue are products
of the author's imagination and are not to be construed as real. Any resemblance to actual people,
living or dead, events or locales is entirely coincidental.

www.holly-webb.com

Chapter One

It was half-past seven on the first morning of the new school year — and things were not going to plan in the Ryan house.

"Mum! Where's my pencil case?"

"And my PE kit?"

"And my other shoe?"

Three excited and slightly panicky voices spoke at once, and Mrs Ryan looked round from the kitchen counter in horror. "What on earth's happened? You had everything yesterday — it can't all have disappeared overnight."

Sometimes, generally when all the floor-space in the house had disappeared under piles of washing, Mrs Ryan wondered how her daughters managed to cause at least ten girls' worth of confusion. What was it about the triplets that made them seem like three blonde hurricanes? She looked at the girls scurrying round the kitchen in a panic and laughed. At least she got more than three times the fun as well!

"Your shoe's there, Becky, under the table, look."

"I definitely didn't leave it there – I wish you'd play football with your *own* shoes, Katie. It's always mine that end up kicked into stupid places."

"I'm *wearing* my shoes, silly. You shouldn't leave them lying around – it's too tempting. Where is that pencil case, I know I had it. . ."

Katie rummaged around on the kitchen table, rooting through Mrs Ryan's newspaper, and threatening to disturb the large pile of her mother's filing that was towering in the middle of the big pine table.

"Oh, Katie, I was reading that! And please

don't knock that pile over, I'd just sorted it – oh, well," Mrs Ryan sighed. "Look – your pencil case is here, in your bag where you put it last night. Honestly, you three, I think you all need glasses. Annabel, what did you say you'd lost?"

"My PE kit, but I haven't, Orlando's sitting on it. Get off, you great lump!"

Annabel tugged at her purple PE bag, trying to dislodge the fat ginger cat who'd decided that her tracksuit and trainers were definitely comfier than his expensive cat basket. Orlando yawned, and stretched, and then shook out his fearsomely clawed paws as slowly as he could. He gave Annabel a look of total contempt and strolled over to Becky to see if he could get a second breakfast out of her.

"Come here, Orlando," said Becky, picking him up and rubbing her face against his ears, starting a rumbling purr from somewhere deep inside him. "Ignore that awful Annabel, she doesn't love you at all, does she?"

"Huh. When that cat apologizes for being sick on my best T-shirt, then I might just decide to like him again. But I'm still waiting. Fleabag!" Annabel hissed, mock-furiously.

Orlando hissed back, and then turned his "I'm starving" face on Becky, and gave a piteous little mew.

"Uh-uh," said Becky. "I'm not falling for it today, puss. I know I've fed you. It's your own fault if you ate the whole bowl in ten seconds flat." She tapped his nose with one finger firmly. "No more food!"

Orlando wriggled crossly till Becky put him down, and then stalked off to sulk in next door's garden. Maybe today would be the day that all his hours of watching their bird table finally paid off.

"Sit down and eat your breakfast, you three. You need to have plenty to keep you going. I should think you'll be running about all over the place," said Mum, sipping her coffee.

"I'm really glad that we went to the Open

4

Evening," said Katie. "At least we know where we're going. I think I do, anyway."

"Well, I can't remember anything," said Annabel. "Except that all the corridors had paint the colour of sick."

"Uurrgh! Bel, that's disgusting. I was going to have some muesli and now you've really put me off." Becky pushed her bowl away, shuddering. Her stomach wasn't happy anyway, as all her nervousness about the new school seemed to be having a party in there, but now she felt even worse.

"I don't know how you can eat that stuff, anyway. It looks *exactly* like the mix you give the guinea pigs. It's probably just the same thing in a different packet."

"Except I think the guinea-pig food costs more," put in Mum. "Your zoo in the shed is eating us out of house and home, Becky."

Becky grinned. She knew Mum didn't mean it. She loved having all the animals around. It wasn't just Orlando and the guinea pigs –

there was Pixie, the little black cat who'd turned up in the garden one morning two years ago, and stayed, and every so often a bird that Becky had rescued, generally from Pixie, who was a ruthless hunter. Becky thought it might be because Pixie had lived as a stray – she wasn't used to two delicious bowls of Whiskas a day, and she liked her food on the move.

"How about some toast instead?" Mum offered.

"OK. I'll put some on – anyone else?" said Becky, jumping up. Perhaps a piece of toast would help her feel less weird.

Annabel looked longingly at the loaf that Becky was waving at her in a tempting fashion. "Nope," she said finally. "Can't manage it."

"I'm not surprised. You practically inhaled that cereal," said Katie. "I'll have some, please, Becky. Can you pass the peanut butter, too?"

Mrs Ryan started to assemble three packed lunches from the fridge. "So you think you know where your classroom is, Katie?" she said.

"Yes, I think so. And the hall. And I definitely know how to get to the playing fields. They looked excellent. Loads more space than our old school. I can't wait."

Annabel looked at her sister sadly. "Mad. Probably got hit on the head by a football – a tragic case."

"Huh. Well, at least I've got some clue where I'm going. Can you remember anything? Oh no, course not – there's no clothes shops at school. And Becky'll only know where there's a bird's nest in the playground. It'll be me looking after the two of you, *as usual*."

Katie was quite right. She was much the most organized of the triplets, and she did tend to lead the other two around. The triplets might look identical, but their characters were totally different. Katie, confident and a bit bossy, Annabel, a head-in-the-clouds, happy-go-lucky show-off, and Becky, the shyest and most thoughtful of the three.

And of course, thought Mrs Ryan, as she surveyed the fridge, *they* would *all like different food*. Had she got it all in the right boxes? One purple and silver lunchbox with cheese sandwiches, one Manchester United lunchbox with ham, and one blue box with a kitten on, with cheese *and* ham. At least they all liked granary bread – this week, anyway!

Mrs Ryan finished her coffee, then noticed the time and panicked. "You'd better have one last check that you've got everything, girls, and then put your jumpers on. It's nearly quarter-past eight."

Becky and Katie licked toast crumbs off their fingers and went to put their plates in the sink.

"Are you working at home today, Mum?" asked Annabel, running her spoon round her cereal bowl for the last few drops of milk. Mrs Ryan worked as a translator, translating books in French and German into English, and the other way round. Most days she worked at home, but about once a week she went into an office. It was a good system, as it meant she was able to fit in work and looking after the triplets.

"Yes, I'll be here all day. I'm in the office for a meeting on Thursday. I've got a lot to do this week."

"Excellent. Does that mean we get to cook dinner?" asked Annabel. She loved to cook – especially cakes that she could decorate afterwards – and then eat! The others loved to cook, too, but it generally ended up with Becky doing the washing up, after Katie had fought with Annabel to try and make her clean up her own mess.

"Mmm, I could certainly do with some help. Of course, I'll have to fit in the shopping first. Any requests?"

"Fish fingers. Can we have them for tonight's tea?" asked Katie.

"We're nearly out of crisps, too. And can we have some more of those minty biscuits?" added Annabel.

"You're such a junk-food freak," said Becky. "Don't forget the cat food this time, Mum."

"Hang on, hang on, I need to write this down. Biscuits, yes," muttered Mrs Ryan, grabbing a pad from by the kitchen phone. "Cat food. . ."

"Come *on*, Mum, if you're sure you really want to come." Katie had her arms folded, and was looking impatient.

"Of course I'm coming with you on your first morning! Get your things together, girls, we'd better be off. Manor Hill is a bit further away than your old school."

"I'm glad we can still walk though," said Katie, closing the front gate behind her, and patting Pixie, who'd managed to squash

10

herself on to the gatepost. "Watch it, Pixie – move one paw a centimetre and you'll be in a real state. I don't know how she can sit there like that – it can't be comfy."

"I think she's just proving she can!" giggled Becky, as they all headed up the road towards their new school.

Chapter Two

Manor Hill School was about two kilometres from the Ryans' house. It was a nice walk, past the park, where the triplets had been going to play on the swings and feed the ducks for as long as they could remember, and then up the high street – definitely Annabel's favourite part of the journey.

"Come on, Bel!" shouted Katie, when she and Becky and Mum realized that they had lost a member of the party. "Look, she's window-shopping at Silver again." Silver was absolutely Annabel's favourite shop. Katie and Becky quite liked it, too, but Annabel would have spent all her pocket money, and all her weekends there, given half a chance.

Silver was mostly a clothes shop, but it also sold fab jewellery and lots of makeup – including nail polish, Annabel's main weakness. Practically her favourite possession was a big, pale pink, circular cardboard box filled with bottles of nail polish, in all colours. Sparkly, scented, glow in the dark – Annabel had them all, plus transfers and nail jewels.

"Bel! We're going to be late if you don't come on!" called Becky. "Let's look on the way home this afternoon."

Annabel reluctantly dragged herself away from the window of Silver and ran to catch up with her sisters. "Sorry! There's such a gorgeous dress in the window. I'll show you later on."

"OK, Becky, it's going to have to be quick march past the pet shop – got it?" said Katie, firmly grabbing her sister's elbow. "We're not being late on the first morning!"

"Oh, that's so unfair!" gasped Becky. "All the animals are inside – even I'm not animal-mad

13

enough to want to look at a hamster-cage display for that long."

"Could have fooled me," said Mrs Ryan cheerfully.

Katie and Annabel laughed, and Becky grinned. "OK, OK, but you never know. We might get a hamster one of these days. I could really fancy having one of those tiny little Russian ones – they are *so* cute."

"Yeah, Orlando and Pixie would love one of those," added Katie. "Well, maybe one each." She dodged out of the way as Becky swung a PE bag at her.

They were getting quite close to Manor Hill by this time, and there were lots of other children around, wearing the same uniform of grey trousers or green checked summer dresses. Even though it was September, it was still summer-hot, and none of the girls wanted to wear the stifling grey skirts and white blouses that were the winter uniform. Well, apart from the older-looking girls stalking past and giving all these new little children disgusted looks. They all looked as though they'd never been seen within ten metres of a checked summer dress. Practically everyone had on the dark green sweatshirt with the red Manor Hill badge in the middle.

The uniform meant that for once the triplets were dressed almost identically. They'd never really been keen on dressing in matching clothes, even when they were quite little. Their grandmothers were always sending them three sets of the same outfit (generally pink, and flouncy) and Mrs Ryan would get them to wear it long enough for a few very sulky photos, and that would be it.

Katie, Becky and Annabel were keeping an eye out for any of their friends from their old school – quite a few were coming to Manor Hill, too. They walked past St Anne's just at the end of the high street. It felt very strange to see all those children going into the playground when the triplets had to walk straight past.

They were starting to feel a tiny bit nervous now, and Annabel looked back at their old school and said, "It's scary. We'll be the youngest ones, the babies. We knew everybody at St Anne's and now we've got to start all over again."

"I know what you mean," Katie answered. "But I think we'll be OK. Remember our first day at St Anne's in the reception class? We were all terrified – you cried."

"I did not! It was Becky!"

"You all did, as far as I can remember," Mrs Ryan intervened. "But don't worry, Annabel. Think of it this way – there'll be some children there who don't know anybody at all. You three have got each other to rely on. But that doesn't mean letting Katie do all the work, you two." Mrs Ryan pointed firmly at Becky and Annabel. "You can all help each other. And then there are all your old friends from St Anne's, too – you're really very lucky."

"I suppose so," said Annabel. "I do wish it

was next week, though. Then we'd have met everybody, and we'd know where things were. I hate having to ask people, it makes me feel so silly."

"And you think you'll know how to get everywhere by next week?" Katie asked disbelievingly. "You'll still be getting lost at the end of term, Bel, you know what you're like."

"Yes, all right," admitted Annabel. "But you know what I mean – by next week we'll kind of know what's going on, who the teachers are, and which ones are nice."

"Our form teacher is new, too, isn't she, Mum?" asked Becky. "She'll be just as lost as we are. That's probably a good thing." She looked round at the swarms of green and grey going past her. How many people would fit into this new school? Somehow, she suspected that not everyone was feeling lost, either. They didn't look it, all talking loudly and chasing after each other.

"You three will have to be careful," warned Mum. "You know some teachers are horrified by the idea of having identical twins in the class – let alone identical triplets. Be on your best behaviour!"

"Yes, Mum," chorused the triplets, grinning at each other. They liked the idea of being a teacher's nightmare. Even Becky felt a bit more cheerful as the triplets imagined their new teachers realizing they had three identical girls in nearly identical uniforms to deal with – this would be fun!

"Hmmm. Well, just remember – I don't want any notes home!"

Three pairs of totally innocent, round blue eyes gazed up at her angelically. "Us?" they seemed to be saying. "Would we?"

Mrs Ryan sighed – after seven weeks of practically non-stop triplets over the summer holidays she had a lot of sympathy for their new school. The staff were in for a shock. Mrs Ryan had a twin sister herself – twins and triplets quite often run in families – and she remembered the mischief that she and her sister Janet had got up to at school.

"Look, we're nearly there," said Becky nervously. The triplets and their mother were part of a flood of children now, all heading for the school gates. Becky looked round – no familiar faces. Manor Hill was quite a large school, drawing pupils from a wide area, and to three brand new year sevens it looked like there were thousands of them, all *huge*.

Suddenly Annabel was waving. "There's Fiona!" she exclaimed happily.

Fiona was a girl the triplets had known at St Anne's – they'd quite often walked to school with her, as she only lived a couple of streets away from them. It made all of the triplets feel a bit better to see at least one other person they knew.

"Right, girls. Are you going to be OK if I leave you here?" asked Mrs Ryan, putting down all the bags she'd been carrying.

"Yes!" gulped Katie, and Becky and Annabel nodded.

"Don't forget – if your teacher gives you any letters to bring home about school trips, or anything like that – I do actually need to see them! I don't want to find them three weeks later in all the grot at the bottom of your schoolbags. Have a good day. Remember what you do so that you can tell me all about it when you get home. I'll see you at about four, yes? Come straight home! Bye darlings!" Mrs Ryan gave each of the girls a big hug, and then turned to go.

Katie, Annabel and Becky watched as she reached the corner of the road and then looked at each other. Then Annabel picked up her bags and said, "OK?"

"OK," the other two answered, and together the Ryan triplets headed into the playground to start their first day at Manor Hill.

Chapter Three

The playground seemed to be entirely full of children dashing about, like a nest of mad bees.

"Come on," decided Katie, taking the lead as usual. "I can't see anyone I know. Let's just go and put our bags down over there, and then we can look for people more easily." She led the way over to a set of steps, which she at least recognized as leading into the dining hall. "Just dump it all here, then we'll go and find everyone – we know Fiona's here somewhere, at least!"

The triplets made a neat pile of their bags and then turned to survey the playground. They didn't realize it at first, but they were getting quite a lot of attention themselves. Their hair was different, but they still looked like the same girl three times over. Children who'd come from different schools whispered to each other, and pointed them out. Becky, who was always the most sensitive, noticed this, and felt embarrassed. The triplets were used to people – usually old ladies – stopping them in the street to ask questions and admire them, but Becky didn't remember quite so many people looking at them at once before. It felt really uncomfortable! She nudged Annabel. "Bel, look! People are staring at us! Those girls over there, do you see? And those two there!"

Annabel peered round carefully, checking out the girls Becky had nodded at, and spotting a few more curious glances on the way. "You're right, Becky. Good. This is going to be fun – I like being noticed!" She preened slightly, and stood up straighter.

Becky sighed. That was just like Annabel. Such a show-off! She watched Annabel tossing her long blonde hair and squirmed inside. It was all right for Bel – she loved attention. Whenever anyone asked her if she knew what she wanted to do when she was older, she always said the same thing, "I'm going to be famous!" Annabel wasn't sure what for yet, but Becky thought she probably would be one day. Bel could be *very* stubborn.

Meanwhile, Katie had finally found some people they knew. A group of children from St Anne's had gathered over by a huge horse chestnut tree in the corner of the playground. The tree had enormous roots that seemed to form little holes and seats, and the St Anne's lot were squashed all round it in a very precarious-looking fashion, obviously swapping gossip from their holidays.

The triplets dashed over, calling to people they knew. Fiona spotted them coming, and waved madly.

Saima bounced up from her seat – nearly knocking Fiona over on the way – and hugged all three triplets in turn. "Oh, I'm so glad to see you – I was so scared when I got to the playground. I couldn't see *anybody* I recognized!"

The triplets nipped back to grab their stuff and then dumped their bags in the teetering pile by the tree and grinned at each other, feeling a little bit silly. Mum was right – it was so much easier for the three of them.

"So come on, Saima, tell us! How was India?" asked Annabel.

"It was brilliant, but it was so hot! I'm just not used to it, I guess. My cousins were running around all over the place, but I could hardly move some days!"

"Did you bring back more gorgeous clothes?" asked Annabel. Saima had shown her some of the beautiful Indian outfits she owned. Lots of them were made of silk, and they were the most amazing colours. They were covered with embroidery, too, and Annabel loved them.

"Yeah, loads. Do you want to come and see them some time?"

"Definitely. Can we dress up in them again? Our dad gave us a digital camera to share – we could take photos," Annabel said excitedly.

"That would be excellent. Oooh, talking of photos, you should see mine, Becky. We saw loads of animals – I was disappointed, though, I was hoping to see a tiger. So, what did you do this summer? Did you go away at all?"

"Yes, Dad took us on holiday – that's when he gave us the camera," answered Becky a bit shyly. She'd never got to know Saima all that well, and found her quite scary – she was always so perfect-looking with her long, glossy black hair and completely immaculate uniform. "It was really cool. We went pony-trekking in Wales for a week. Not quite as exciting as India, though."

"Yeah, and my bottom still hasn't recovered. Saddles are really, really hard!" cut in Annabel. "But Becky's right, it was so cool. We had the same pony each for the whole week. Mine was black and he was called Jet. He was really naughty, though. Every time we went past anything eatable-looking – nice flowers, or leaves, or someone's packed lunch – it was straight into his mouth. I kept having to pull him away."

"And it was great to see Dad," added Katie. "It felt like ages since we'd had any time with him."

Saima nodded sympathetically – she knew that the triplets' dad was an engineer, and he worked abroad for long periods of time. It was part of the reason he and their mum had split up. "Has he gone back to Egypt now?" she asked.

"Yes, unfortunately," groaned Katie. "He's working on an irrigation project, and they're really behind schedule. It could be a while before he's back here again. He emails us lots, though, and we can skype him.

"But apart from that week, we stayed at

home," explained Annabel. "It wasn't very exciting. In a way it's quite nice to be back at school."

Everyone gave Annabel a look of horror.

"Don't look at me like that! I just mean that being at home was getting quite boring. It would have been OK if the weather was better, but it was totally grim. We were really lucky to get sunshine the week we were in Wales. Weren't we?" She nudged Katie, who clearly wasn't listening. Some boys that the triplets didn't know had started a football game in the middle of the playground, piling up jackets for the goals. Katie was watching them longingly. Annabel laughed. "OK, there's no point talking to Katie, not now there's a football in sight."

It was very unlikely that the boys would let Katie join in, but she was sure she could play better than most of them. Look at that dark-haired one, for instance. His shots were going completely wide every time. He seemed to be a very selfish player, too – he kept hogging the ball and trying to shoot, even though his mates were yelling at him to pass. Katie itched to get up and tackle him. She didn't quite dare, though. Maybe in a couple of weeks' time she might know them enough to ask if she could play. For the moment she just sat tight and watched with a *very* critical eye.

Suddenly the dark-haired boy lost control of the ball entirely and booted it off the "pitch", straight towards where the triplets and their friends were sitting. Fiona had to dodge backwards, and as it was the ball only just missed her glasses. It ended up practically at Becky's feet.

"Hey, watch it!" Katie yelled to the dark-haired boy. "You could have hurt somebody!"

"Stupid girls!" he snapped back at her. "You shouldn't have been in the way."

The whole group round the tree gasped with indignation – how dare he! It had been completely his fault, and now he was trying to blame them! For once, Katie was speechless, and the boy rolled his eyes in disgust, propped his hands on his hips and turned on Becky. "Come on then," he spat, "kick it back, you dumb blonde!"

Becky seemed to be frozen. She absolutely *hated* people staring at her and now it seemed as if the whole playground was watching. She was petrified of doing something wrong, making herself – and her sisters – look silly and causing this horrible boy to shout at her even more. She just couldn't make herself kick the ball, even though she knew how easy it was.

The boy glared at her. "Come on, stupid!" he yelled. "Kick it!" Then he sighed, seemed to give up on Becky ever plucking up the courage to move, and headed towards the girls to fetch the ball himself.

By this time, though, Katie was seething. How could this horrible boy yell at her sister – especially when he'd nearly hit Fiona, and not even bothered to apologize. She grabbed the ball with both hands and threw it at him, pushing it as hard as she could, and aiming it perfectly. It hit him right in the stomach – just where Katie had meant it to – and knocked the breath out of him. Katie followed the ball up to the boy and stood glaring at him as he gasped for air. She jabbed her finger in his chest and snarled, "Don't you ever speak to my sister like that again, you idiot – and why don't you learn to kick a ball properly!" Then she calmly collected the ball, which was on the ground next to the idiot boy (with her left foot, she was showing off a bit), and booted it with all her strength straight between the two piles of jackets, leaving the boys gobsmacked. She smirked at them all, turned, and headed back to her friends by the tree.

"Wow, Katie!" gasped Annabel. "That was brilliant! You really showed him!"

"Thanks, Katie," whispered Becky, who was still looking really upset.

Katie put an arm round Becky and squeezed her tight. "You mustn't listen to idiots like him, Becky," she said, turning to look back at the boys, who were just starting their game again, although the dark-haired boy didn't seem to be joining in much. "He's just a stupid, loud-mouthed moron and you can't let him upset you."

"She's right. I know you, Becky, you'll worry about it all day – you just forget him," added Annabel, coming up on Becky's other side and hugging her too.

Becky nodded, and smiled at her sisters, grateful for their hugs and encouraging words. It was hard, though. Bel and Katie were so much more confident than she was – and she didn't think they understood that. That boy had made her feel small and stupid, and she wished she could just go home.

Katie put her hands on Becky's shoulders and gave her a little shake. "C'mon! Smile properly!" she coaxed, and was rewarded with a bigger smile this time, as Becky tried hard to forget her bruised feelings.

Suddenly the bell rang, and several more teachers came out into the playground. One of them blew a whistle, and started to call out class names and point to teachers. Soon everyone was heading into the school – it was time for the triplets to meet their new class teacher.

Chapter Four

Miss Fraser, the school's new history teacher, and the triplets' class teacher, looked nice. She seemed very young, and had really pretty red curly hair and lots of freckles, especially on her arms. She also looked quite nervous – twenty-eight pairs of eyes were watching her with interest as she picked up the register. She started to work her way through the list of names, looking up and smiling as each member of her class answered. When she got to the Ryans she looked faintly worried. "I knew we had triplets in this class, but I didn't imagine you'd look quite so alike. . ."

"Don't worry, Miss Fraser," Katie reassured her. "We always wear our hair differently."

Miss Fraser looked carefully at the triplets and felt slightly relieved. It was true — their long golden-blonde hair *was* different. Becky had two long bunches, Katie had hers plaited quite tightly out of the way, and Annabel looked completely the opposite, with her hair loose and just a couple of glittery clips holding it off her face.

Annabel smiled at Miss Fraser. "Almost always, anyway," she said.

Miss Fraser finished the register, and explained that for most of that morning everyone would stay in their form room to work out timetables and get all their books. Proper lessons wouldn't start until that afternoon. She passed out labels that fitted into the slots on the lockers where they'd keep their books, and told the class that their first job was to decorate their labels. The triplets were sitting with Fiona and Saima, and they chatted as they passed round felt-tips. Katie whispered to Annabel, nodding towards the other side of the classroom. "Look – don't tell Becky, but that stupid boy's over there. We'll have to keep an eye on him," she said seriously.

Annabel peered round. Katie was right – well, perhaps they could avoid him? She just had a horrible feeling it wasn't going to be that easy.

"So what do you think of Miss Fraser so far?" Saima asked, smiling directly at Becky, so she felt she had to answer.

Becky went pink, and stammered, "I don't know really. I'm just glad we're all three in the same class – I was worried they might split us up."

"Mmmm," agreed Katie, "that would have been a bit weird. I don't know if they'd do that, though, would they? Anyway, we were really glad when we got that letter saying we were all in Miss Fraser's class."

Becky tried hard not to look upset. *A bit weird?* Was that really what Katie thought, or was she being Katie-ish, and trying to sound grown-up? As far as Becky was concerned it would have been more like a total and utter disaster, not just a bit weird.

"I think Miss Fraser's nice," Fiona put in. "It's really good to have young teachers – I think they're more interesting."

"Mmm," said Annabel thoughtfully. "She was a bit thrown by us three, though, wasn't she? She didn't look at all happy."

"Well, Mum said that might happen," said Katie. "We'll just have to be little angels for a couple of weeks, to convince her we're not going to be any trouble."

"Do you really think so?" Annabel sounded disappointed. "I thought we could give her till break to sort out which of us has which hairstyle – and then we could swap round. She'd be completely mixed up!" Annabel's eyes sparkled at the thought.

"No!" squeaked Becky in horror.

"On the first day?" added Katie. "You must be mad, Bel. No. Way."

Annabel sighed disappointedly. "Oh, I suppose you're right. But promise me we'll do something like that soon." Annabel was definitely the most daring of the triplets. She had a habit of doing things that sounded fun, and then only realizing afterwards that it might not have been such a good idea. But then, as Katie always pointed out disgustedly, she was also incredibly lucky, and generally managed to get away with whatever it was by looking angelic, and giving the impression that it was all a mistake and she had no idea how it had happened. Katie didn't have the knack, so her reply wasn't encouraging:

"*Maybe.* We don't know what Miss Fraser's like yet. If she's really strict then it's stupid to get ourselves into trouble. Don't you think so, Becky?"

"Yes. If she's nice and she'll just think we're funny, then OK. But not for a while. Anyway, we ought to check out the other teachers first," said Becky, trying to calm her sisters down.

Annabel was looking huffy, and the argument might have carried on, but Miss Fraser told everyone to stick their labels on to their lockers and put their new books in. Then she dictated their timetable to them, and they tried to decipher the little maps of the school that they'd been given.

It was very hard to sit still and concentrate after seven weeks of summer holidays – and the playground looked amazingly inviting. As soon as the bell went the entire class jumped to their feet, desperate to get out into the fresh air after the stuffy classroom. Just as the triplets reached the door, though, Miss Fraser called them back.

"Girls! Could I have a word, please?"

Annabel wasn't listening, and she was already dashing out of the door – she always had hated sitting still! Katie had to chase after her to bring her back.

"I'm sorry, Miss Fraser, I didn't hear you," she panted.

"I won't keep you a minute, girls. I just need to have a quick chat with you." Miss Fraser seemed to be a little lost for words. "It's ... very exciting having triplets in the class, but I think it's important that you don't stick with each other all the time. It'll be easier for you to make new friends that way. So, when I split this class up into groups for our history project–work – well, I think we might have to separate you. I imagine some of the other teachers might do the same."

"You mean we can't work together?" said Becky, sounding worried.

"Well, I really think it would be easier for everyone if you didn't," said Miss Fraser briskly. "I should think it might be good for you three to learn to work with other people, as well. Don't look so worried!" She smiled at Becky, who was nibbling her nails. "You'll be fine. Off you go outside now. Get some fresh air."

The triplets traipsed outside slowly, and

stood just outside the main door, looking thoughtfully at each other.

"Wow," said Katie. "I wasn't expecting that. I think she might be stricter than she looks."

"What are we going to do?" Becky felt panicky, almost as though she might cry. She couldn't believe it! After what Katie had said in the classroom just before, it seemed like some kind of horrible sign that they were going to be split up after all.

"Do?" asked Annabel. "What do you mean? I guess we'll just be in separate groups, like she said. It's not for the whole time, Becky. Just for one subject."

"Cheer up, Becky. It'll be fine, like Miss Fraser said, we'll get to know some new people." Katie nudged her with an elbow. "You look as if you're about to be sick."

The awful thing was, Becky almost did feel as though she might be! The day just seemed to be getting worse and worse. Didn't Katie and Annabel *care* that they were going to be split up? And what if all the other teachers did the same? Becky couldn't imagine being apart from her sisters – they were always together.

"C'mon. Let's go and find Fiona and Saima," suggested Annabel, and she and Katie led the way over to the big chestnut tree, which seemed to have become their friends' pet place.

"What did Miss Fraser want?" asked Saima with interest, when they got there. "You're not in trouble already, are you?"

"Course not," laughed Katie. "Though, actually, with Annabel, you never can tell. No, she just wanted to tell us we won't always be allowed to sit together in class."

"Yeah, we've got to do some sort of project-work, and we've got to be in different groups. Actually, Saima, maybe we could be in a group together?" Annabel suggested.

Saima looked pleased. "OK – yes, that would be cool."

Fiona, who was a noticing kind of person,

looked carefully at Becky as she asked, "And that's OK with all of you? You don't mind being separated?"

Becky spotted that look, though the others didn't seem to have done, and gave Fiona a quick smile. No way was she going to make a fuss about this if the other two weren't bothered. "It'll be different," she said, shrugging. "That's all."

Luckily for Becky, something rather strange happened then, which distracted everybody. One of the girls in their class, who'd come from a different school, wandered past the little group by the tree in a casual-but-obviously-on-purpose way. She was very pretty, as distinctive-looking as the triplets, really, with wavy strawberry-blonde hair worn loose like Annabel's, and nearly long enough to sit on. Following her were two other girls, obviously worshipping the ground she walked on. As they went past, all three of them quite clearly sneered.

"Well!" said Saima. "What was all that about? Do you know them?"

"Nope," said Annabel, confused. "She's in our class, isn't she? And the other two, I think." She shrugged. "Weird. Never mind. Anyone know what's happening after break?"

Just then the bell went, and they found out – assembly, which was basically a lecture on the school rules. There seemed to be millions of them, and by lunchtime everyone was worried about doing *anything* in case a teacher swooped out of nowhere to give them a detention for it. Becky's sick feeling was still there, in fact it seemed to be getting worse, and she couldn't even tell anyone about it.

After lunch in the dining hall (where the triplets had to swap their sandwiches round as usual – why was it that Mum just couldn't get her head round which of them liked what?) they went off to look at the playing fields, which Katie was still longing to try out! Luckily, Year

Seven's first PE lesson was that afternoon, so she didn't have long to wait.

Manor Hill had several staff to teach PE, and it was Mrs Ross who came to fetch the girls in their class that afternoon to take them to the changing rooms. She seemed fun, and even Becky was feeling chirpier by the time they'd got out to the playing fields. Katie was positively jumping up and down with enthusiasm, especially as Mrs Ross had told them that they'd be doing ball skills today. She and Saima were lugging a big net full of brand-new-looking footballs, and various other members of the class were carrying traffic cones. The boys, who were heading out to the field as well, mostly seemed to be wearing the traffic cones on their heads. This seemed to involve weird *whooargh* noises as well, but none of the girls could see why.

"Right," called Mrs Ross. "Put the cones over here, in a line, that's right. Lovely. Now, an orderly queue, please, and we're going to practise dribbling through the cones. Who wants to go first?"

Everyone shuffled their feet a bit, and avoided looking at Mrs Ross, so she picked a girl that the triplets didn't know. She looked terribly embarrassed, and unfortunately managed to trip over her feet and knock two of the cones over halfway round. Almost everyone pretended not to notice – they were too busy being glad they hadn't had to go first to laugh. The girl with the strawberry-blonde hair and her two little mates had their sneering faces on again, though. When it got to Katie's turn, Mrs Ross got very excited. Katie had been to a soccer summer school, and done lots of this sort of thing. She moved round the cones amazingly fast, expertly dribbling the ball from foot to foot as the rest of the class watched open-mouthed. From the other side of the field, the dark-haired boy who'd been so horrible that morning looked very sulky indeed as Mrs Ross enthused about Katie's flying feet.

After that they practised kicking the ball backwards and forwards in pairs, trying to keep it under control. Katie's partner was called Megan. She wasn't bad at football herself, but she explained she preferred being a goalie. She was very impressed with Katie's ball skills and Katie showed her a clever trick she'd learned at the summer school, using the side of her foot to get the ball going exactly where she wanted it.

Annabel and Becky were paired together, and had a good time – quite a lot of it spent chasing the ball when it went wide, but they still had fun. The running about seemed to blow away the stuffy feeling of the classroom, and by the end of the lesson practically everyone was feeling ready for a sit-down; even if it had to be sitting down doing maths.

Their new maths teacher, Mr Jones (definitely not one to mess with – not yet, anyway – the triplets decided) made no allowances for it being the first day. It was straight into revision of long multiplication and division, strictly no calculators allowed. Katie was galloping through the problems on the board (Becky and Annabel chewed their pencils and sighed – Katie was unfairly good at maths, and Mr Jones would be bound to think they could do it, too) when the loud shrill of the bell interrupted – it was the end of their first day!

Chapter Five

The cloakroom was a mad scrimmage as everyone fought to be first out of the school gates. Eventually, though, the triplets got their stuff together and headed off home. They were just turning into the high street when they spotted a familiar figure.

"Mum!" said Katie in surprise. "What are you doing here? You were supposed to wait for us at home."

"Oh, I know," agreed Mrs Ryan, "but I just couldn't – I was sitting there worrying, not getting any work done. I wanted to know how your first day had gone, so I thought I'd meet you halfway." She noted Katie's scowl. "I'm sorry, Katie – you really wanted to walk home on your own, didn't you?"

"Don't be such a grump!" Annabel told her sister.

Becky put her arm through Mum's. She couldn't believe how much better it made her feel to see her. Mum was great at making you feel loved, and Becky felt like she needed that just now.

"Sorry, Mum," said Katie, not sounding particularly sorry. "But you did say we could go home on our own – we're not little any more! We're at secondary school now, it's different."

Annabel nodded, serious for once. "She's right, Mum."

Both Katie and Annabel sounded almost eager for things to change, thought Becky, squeezing Mum's arm and feeling the hole that had been growing in the middle of her stomach all day get a bit bigger.

"It's so good to see you!" she burst out, and Mum looked down at her, slightly worried. "But Katie's right," Becky added quickly, not wanting Mum and the others to know what she was really feeling. "We can definitely walk home on our own now."

"Well, I promise it was just this once," said Mum apologetically. "Now, please, put me out of my misery – tell me what it was like! Becky, how did it go?"

Becky summoned a bright smile from somewhere, a kind of emergency back-up smile, and said determinedly, "It was fine. Different, but fine. Really."

Katie gave up looking cross and started to tell Mum about the PE lesson as they walked home. "Manor Hill's got a girls' football team, Mum!" she chattered excitedly. "Well, two, really, but this is the junior one. And Mrs Ross – that's our PE teacher, she's really nice – said that she was looking for people to be on it, and she'd be keeping an eye on me! They play lots of games against other school teams. It would be so excellent to be on a proper football team!"

"Katie, that's wonderful. Well done," said Mum in a delighted voice. "Does that mean I'm going to be standing on a freezing football pitch all winter watching you?"

"Definitely!" Katie grinned. "And you two'll come and watch as well, won't you, if I really get on the team?"

"Course we will, silly!" said Becky.

Annabel looked thoughtful. "We could be your cheerleaders! I'm sure we could make some pompoms easily!"

"*No*, thank you! You don't get cheerleaders at football, Bel! You'll just have to come and yell at the ref like everyone else. And can you imagine how cold you'd be on that football pitch in a cheerleader's outfit in December?"

"They're ever so pretty, though, those little skirts. I've seen them on TV. I'd look nice in one of those, I think," called Annabel, as she went twirling off down the pavement, making up a cheerleader-ish dance and waving her schoolbag in a vaguely pompom-like way. She stopped outside the window of Silver, and beckoned to her sisters. "Look! That's the dress I was talking about this morning. Isn't it gorgeous? I love those glittery beads."

Katie and Becky caught up with her. "Oooh, yes!" agreed Becky. "That's really pretty. Fab colour." It was a short dress in a satiny, pale-blue fabric, with twinkly silver beads round the neck and the hemline.

Mum gazed into the window thoughtfully. "Oh yes, that is nice. Well, I don't think I can quite run to buying dresses today, but why don't we go in and have a look? Maybe you should each have a little something – to celebrate your first day at Manor Hill!"

"Oh, Mum! Thanks!" "Excellent!" "Come on, let's go in!" came the excited chorus from the triplets, and Annabel pushed the door open.

Silver was a treasure-trove of gorgeous stuff, and the girls rushed here and there, darting back to show the best things to their mum. After a little while, Katie decided on a little ring with a purple stone in it. Being a definite jeans person, she didn't wear jewellery very often – but it was nice to have it so you could really dress up sometimes. Becky had found a perfect present for herself – a pendant like a silvery cat's face, with tiny green jewels for the eyes. She was convinced it looked just like Pixie. Only Annabel was left, wavering between some nail polish that somehow – no one was quite sure how – had two colours in the same bottle, so that you got a marbled effect when you put it on your nails, or a pair of hairgrips shaped like pink butterflies. In the end she went for the hairgrips – but she knew she'd be back for that nail polish pretty soon.

Mum paid for their presents, and then they headed on home. She had just managed to find time to fit in the shopping, but once the triplets were home, they got the impression she might have been worrying about how they were doing at school while she was wandering around the supermarket as well.

"Mum, where did you put the cat food?" asked Becky, ransacking the cupboard.

"Oh! Cat food!" squeaked Mrs Ryan in horror. "I knew there was something. Oh, Becky, I'm sorry!"

Annabel and Katie, who were sitting on the kitchen counter examining the slightly random stuff that their mother had bought, rolled their eyes at each other. Becky grinned and went back to the cupboard, which was a bit of a black hole. At last she discovered a tin of the cats' least favourite brand lurking behind the orange squash. Orlando and Pixie's whiskers drooped in disbelief.

Mum still had some work to finish off – she really had been worrying about them, and it felt nice. She promised tea soon, if they'd just let her have half an hour. The triplets changed out of their uniform into comfy clothes and curled up on the sofa to watch TV – with the packet of minty biscuits that Mum had luckily remembered to buy! They didn't have any homework to do – none of the teachers had been that cruel. So they looked forward to an evening of just recovering from school. Although, looking at Katie and Annabel, Becky wondered why she felt like she had to do so much more recovering than they did. School had been an ordeal, and she was hugely relieved it was over. The only problem was, she had to go back tomorrow, and keep on pretending that she liked it. Or at least that it wasn't making her feel hollow inside. Katie and Annabel didn't look hollow at all – they were practically bouncy.

The triplets had half an eye on the TV, and most of their attention on the horoscopes in Annabel's *Girl Talk* magazine when the phone rang. Katie jumped, and considered making a dash for it, but then remembered that Mum was in the kitchen working, practically next to the phone. They all listened carefully, though, to see if it was one of their mum's friends, or something to do with them. Their mum sounded pleased to hear from whoever it was. "Oh, hello! Well remembered. Yes, I'm sure they'd love to talk to you, Dan."

Dan! It was their dad!

The triplets looked at each other in delight, and then there was an undignified scramble off the sofa to get to the kitchen and speak to him.

Mum laughed. "Can you hear the approaching herd of elephants, Dan?" She handed the phone to the triplets, who huddled round it excitedly, all desperate to hear him. "Here," Mum said, reaching over to press a button. "Put it on speakerphone – then at least you can all hear, and you'll just have to take it in turns to talk!"

"Hello, loves!" came their dad's voice down the line – everybody jumped. Dad was shouting, as it wasn't a very clear line, and that made him very loud on the speakerphone.

"How was your first day? I'm really sorry, I can't be too long as I'm supposed to be going to a meeting, but I just wanted to let you know I was thinking about you! What was it like?"

"It was great, Dad!" gabbled Katie in excitement. "I might get to be on the football team!"

"Fantastic! That's my girl. All that practice in the park paid off, then! How about you, Becky? All the animals OK? Meet any nice animal-mad friends today?"

"The pets are all fine, Dad. We didn't meet that many new people today, but we saw Saima and Fiona — you remember them?"

"Yes, of course. How about you, Annabel, sweetheart? Keeping out of trouble?"

"Yep, so far. I really want to try and put one over on our class teacher, though. But the other two won't let me."

"Totally unfair of them, Bel. Give it time, though, I'm sure you'll win them over."

Katie and Becky exchanged looks. It was

just like Dad to agree with Bel. They were very alike in some ways, both with a kind of daredevil streak in them. Dad kept his hidden most of the time, though.

"How's your work going, Dad?" asked Becky.

"Urrgh." Mr Ryan heaved a huge sigh. "Slowly, I'm afraid. We really are behind schedule on this one. But we're catching up. Anyway, I'm sorry, I'm going to have to go into that meeting now. Love you loads, and speak soon! Don't forget to send me lots of emails, and some more photos of you all. Say bye to your mum for me!"

"Bye, Dad!" chorused the triplets.

Everyone felt a bit flat after Dad had gone. Speaking to him on the phone or on Skype was a real treat, but it made them realize just how far away he was – *and* how long it would be before they saw him again.

"Come on," said Mum, briskly. "You lot volunteered to help me with the tea this morning. It's fish fingers, I *did* manage to remember those, even though I was thinking about you three instead of my list – can you get them out of the freezer for me, Katie? Top shelf. And there are some frozen peas in there too."

The girls bustled around, Katie arranging fish fingers on an oven tray – and then taking them off again when Mum pointed out that she needed to grease it first.

"*Katie!*" said her sisters disapprovingly.

"Oh, as if you haven't done exactly the same thing!" protested Katie indignantly. "Remember those pizzas, Bel? It took us ages to pick charred pizza off those baking trays." She wiped some vegetable oil round the tray, and replaced the fish fingers. "There! Shall I put the oven on, Mum?"

When everything was ready, Mrs Ryan sat down to chat with the triplets as they munched away. Teatimes were one of the things she wasn't laid-back about. They always ate round the table, and only as a special treat could they take their plates into the living room to watch TV.

"So, tell me some more about school. Did you have lots of different teachers today?"

"A few," said Annabel. "Oooh, we forgot to tell you. Our class teacher's not going to let us sit with each other!"

Becky jumped in. "That's not true, Bel, thank goodness!"

"Yeah, she's exaggerating, Mum," added Katie. "Miss Fraser just said she'd split us up for history projects. We can still sit together in *most* of our lessons."

"Well, that sounds very sensible of Miss Fraser." Mum nodded. "Yes, I think if I were one of your teachers, I might well do the same thing. And it'll be good for you three to make new friends." Mum eyed Becky thoughtfully as she said this. She'd been quiet all evening, and her mum hoped it was just first-day nerves, and not anything more serious. Becky was definitely a little shy – it *would* be good for her to find new friends to work with. As long as she didn't just decide to hide away like a little mouse. . .

Chapter Six

By the time it got to Wednesday, the triplets felt like they'd been back at school for weeks. It was as if the summer holidays had never happened. Becky still wasn't enjoying it much, but at least nothing disastrous had happened, so far. . .

On Wednesday afternoon, they had their first proper history lesson, a double period. Miss Fraser explained that they were going to start a special project that would go on for the next few weeks. It was going to be about their town and its history. The triplets looked worriedly at each other. It sounded like this would be where Miss Fraser got them to work separately. While everyone was muttering about projects being boring and just an excuse for extra homework, Miss Fraser leant over the triplets' table. "OK, you three. We're going to work in groups of four for this project – I'd like you to be in different groups, please." Then she explained to everyone that they could choose their own groups of four, but that if their groups weren't well-balanced, she'd swap them around. No one was entirely sure what well-balanced meant – but they guessed they'd find out.

Becky's hollow-stomach feeling came back with a vengeance as Annabel chirped, "See you later!" and bounced over to Saima, grinning. "Shall we start a group, then?" she suggested.

"OK," agreed Saima, happily. "We can't have your sisters, though, can we?" She smiled at Becky, who was still sitting frozen to her chair. "Shall we ask Fiona? And you know Moira from down my road, don't you? What about her?"

"I don't know," replied Annabel thoughtfully. "I've got a horrible feeling that Miss Fraser wants girls and boys mixed, or she'll make us change. It might be better to start off with boys in our group – at least *we* won't get split up and put with people we don't know."

"Good idea. Who is there we know? Matthew's OK." They knew Matthew from St Anne's; he was very funny. "How about we ask him and Jordan?" Saima jerked her thumb at the boys.

Annabel nodded, and Becky watched as Saima and her sister wandered over in a slightly embarrassed way. Luckily Matthew spotted them.

"Hey, you two! Do you want to be a four with me and Jordan? I thought you'd be with your sisters though, Annabel?"

"Not allowed. Yeah, OK. We don't mind being in a group with you, do we, Saima?" answered Annabel, grinning meaningfully.

Becky's shoulders sagged. She'd tensed

herself up without noticing, hoping that somehow Annabel wouldn't be able to find a group she wanted to be with. Then, according to Becky's imaginary plan, Annabel would beg Miss Fraser to change her mind and let them be together after all. It was what Becky desperately wanted to do herself, but she'd never dare. She'd been relying on Annabel to do it for her, but looking at her bubbly, outgoing sister laughing and chatting with Saima and the boys, she knew how stupidly she'd been deceiving herself.

She got up – she couldn't stay sitting there like an idiot, much as she'd like to – and looked round for Katie, a tiny thread of hope still running through her. Katie was with Fiona, and Moira, the girl Saima had suggested to Annabel. The other person in their group – who was it? Then Becky vaguely recalled her from their PE lesson – Megan, who Katie had said was good at football. So Katie was sorted as well – it was only Becky who was on her own.

Becky chewed her bottom lip thoughtfully. But Katie's group was all girls! Becky was pretty sure Annabel had been right about Miss Fraser wanting mixed groups, so maybe Katie's group would get split up and – surely somehow they'd end up together? Or even if it was only Fiona she was with, at least she knew her. Becky was about to nip over and explain to Katie that she was going to have to change things round somehow, when Miss Fraser interrupted.

"Are we all sorted now? Anyone not in a group?"

"We've only got three, Miss Fraser," called a pretty, dark-haired girl with huge green eyes.

"Oh. Has one group got five?" asked Miss Fraser, looking round.

"No, sorry, Miss Fraser," stammered Becky. "It's me – I'll. . . I'll join this group."

Everyone was looking at her! Oh, why hadn't she got up and done something earlier, made an effort to ask Fiona if she'd be in a group with her? Why did she just have to sit there and let everything go wrong? She couldn't look at Katie and Annabel. She knew Katie would be cross with her for being a baby, and Annabel just wouldn't understand how Becky could manage to be so useless. She had loads of friends – surely Becky could have managed one! Although Becky was mostly feeling really embarrassed about her own complete wimpishness, there was also a niggling hurt lurking in the back of her mind, that Annabel and Katie had just disappeared off without even thinking to ask if she'd be OK.

Katie and Annabel exchanged shocked glances across the room. Becky had been doing a panicky kind of hover at the edge of the room, and neither of them had realized that she was on her own. Now they felt guilty – Katie especially, because she was so used to looking after Bel *and* Becky. She felt a bit cross, though, too. Why hadn't Becky made more of an effort? She couldn't watch out for her sisters *all* the time!

The girl with the long strawberry-blonde hair – they'd worked out that she was called Amy by now, and her two followers were Emily and Cara – watched all this with slightly narrowed eyes. So the practically perfect triplets were being split up, were they? She gazed thoughtfully at Becky, noting her miserable look, and smirked. Definitely information worth having. She turned back to her own group (their fourth person was a boy called David who'd moved into the area that summer and knew nobody – Miss Fraser had put him in their group, and they were intending to ignore him as much as possible) and started planning to herself.

Becky moved over to the green-eyed girl and her friends, looking at the floor, and blushing bright scarlet. Everyone in the class thought she was an idiot, now.

"Hello. Which triplet are you? I'm Fran, by the way." At least the girl with the green eyes seemed friendly, although the two boys were smirking a bit. "This is Jack and Robin. We know each other from our old school."

"Becky," Becky gasped out. "Sorry – Miss Fraser split me and my sisters up. I didn't really know anyone else." Then she blushed an even darker red and closed her mouth, fully intending not to say anything else for the rest of the afternoon, if possible. If she shut up, perhaps they might forget she was there. . .

"Now, this is no good," said Miss Fraser, examining the class. "We can't have you girls all together – and, yes, look, a group of just boys."

Annabel had been right about the mixed groups. Unfortunately, though, she and Becky hadn't realized the worst of it. Miss Fraser did split Katie's group up – she and Megan were with two of the boys. The real problem was, Katie was now condemned to doing a history project with the incredibly annoying boy from Monday morning's football game. He turned out to be called Max.

Chapter Seven

Becky got through the rest of the lesson by withdrawing into a shell like a tortoise. She didn't say *anything*, except once – "Mm" when Fran asked if she was OK. As she was staring at the table top, she didn't see the boys exchange long-suffering looks. Just their luck to be stuck in a group with the mad triplet. The only thing that made Becky feel slightly better was that at least she didn't seem to be in a group with anyone she knew was really horrible (although she might have felt differently if she'd seen Jack and Robin's look). Poor Katie! Becky felt quite seriously that she would actually have died if she'd had to work with that awful boy, Max. The thing was, though, she definitely felt ever so sorry for Katie, but a teensy part of her couldn't help thinking that it served her sister right. A bit.

On the way home from school the triplets carefully ignored the subject of Becky's project group. Becky definitely didn't want to talk about it, and Katie and Bel didn't want to upset her by asking her if she was OK with it — what would they do if she wasn't? It felt strange. None of them were used to having something they couldn't talk about. Instead they concentrated on sympathizing with Katie for her terrible luck.

The weird feeling between the three of them made the next day at school seem really odd. Becky was sure she only survived by repeating to herself over and over again that it was Thursday and there was only one more day to go. Miss Fraser's class was due to have a lesson working on their history projects the next morning — only Annabel thought she might actually enjoy it.

*

Katie got up on Friday without having to be chivvied by Mum, and got dressed feeling almost vicious. She brushed her hair without considering the knots, and winced. Then she plaited it back particularly tightly, thinking that if that boy *dared* say anything she'd . . . well, something, anyway. Mum noticed that breakfast was rather silent, but nothing was obviously wrong – the triplets just seemed to be thoughtful. Although, was she imagining it, or was Becky even quieter than normal?

"Becky, darling, eat that toast – it'll get cold," she pointed out.

Becky looked at the limp slice she'd been ignoring, and sighed. She wasn't hungry, but she didn't feel like explaining why to Mum. This was when she could really do with a dog. Cats were no good in this situation. She didn't think that even Orlando the ever-starving would get rid of a piece of soggy toast for her. Possibly if she put some Marmite on it? Thoughtfully, still pondering how to get a cat

72

to dispose of her breakfast, she took a bite. She was halfway down the slice before she realized what she was doing, and then she decided she might as well finish it.

There was another football game going on in the playground that morning, and Katie, her sisters and Megan watched critically. Katie and Megan had their arms folded, and carefully arranged pitying looks on their faces as they watched Max's game.

"You'd better be careful, Katie," said Becky, worriedly. "You've got to work with him, and his friend – what's he called?"

"Ben. And I don't mind him so much – look, at least he doesn't think he's David Beckham." Katie nodded towards the "pitch", where Ben was capably passing the ball, without trying to do anything too fancy.

When it came to the history lesson, everyone got into their groups with varying degrees of enthusiasm. They were in yet another new classroom – half the class turned up late and looking sheepish, having gone to completely the wrong side of the building and interrupted Year Nine Geography. Looking round at the seven groups, Annabel reckoned that she and Saima had done rather well.

"Do you have any idea what we're supposed to be doing for this project?" Matthew muttered to them.

"Nope," Annabel hissed back cheerfully. "Haven't a clue." Miss Fraser had read them something out of the textbook about research in the last lesson after they'd sorted their groups, but the triplets had still been so focused on being split up that they hadn't really paid much attention. None of the others seemed to have either. . .

"It's history," Jordan chipped in brightly.

Matthew gave him a look. "Yeah, thanks Jordan. Helpful!"

"Well, we never know with you, Matt. I

wouldn't be all that surprised if you turned in a maths project."

Miss Fraser had lots of books about local history, and photocopies of things like the school's record books, old photographs, maps – loads of stuff. That afternoon they were just going to be "sifting through the evidence" as she put it, but eventually they would have to produce a piece of work based on what they'd found out.

The lesson was quite relaxed and cheerful – everyone was wandering around, borrowing books from different tables, giggling at the solemn, old-fashioned-looking children in the old school photos. Miss Fraser seemed to have a laid-back Friday feeling about her, too.

Katie's table, however, was noticeably uncheerful. She and Megan were looking snootily down their noses at Max, and he was glaring back, while poor Ben tried very hard to interest them all in the stuff he'd found to look at for their project. "Look! It says here our school's over a hundred years old!"

"Typical," snapped Max. "*We're* doing all the work while you girls sit around doing nothing."

Even Ben looked a bit gobsmacked by this – Max hadn't done anything!

Katie positively bristled. "Oh, is that right? Well, me and Megan are just going to have to redo all your work anyway, 'cause it'll be useless!"

Max blustered. "Yeah, well, what about you and your stupid sisters! That one" – he nodded to Becky, sitting with Fran's group with her elbows tucked into her sides as if she was trying to make herself so small that no one would notice her – "she's so brainless, she can't even kick a ball!"

Becky heard. Katie could tell that she had, because, impossibly, she seemed to shrink even more. Katie, by contrast, swelled up with fury. But she smiled sweetly at Max. He'd given her the perfect opening for one of the insults she'd considered while brushing her hair that morning. "Oh," she cooed, dangerously, "and you actually think you *can*?"

It was unfortunate that Ben giggled. He tried not to, but Max looked so funny, scowling, and opening and shutting his mouth like a goldfish while he tried to think of an answer. That was all Max needed to lose his temper completely. He stood up, and shoved Ben's pile of books at Katie, who dodged so they went on the floor. Then he turned round to storm away from the table – only he stormed right into Miss Fraser instead. She had seen the books hit the floor and she was *not* happy. Max spent morning break tidying the stationery cupboard. It wasn't even very untidy, but it seemed to be all Miss Fraser could think of. So he actually spent the time sulking, and trying desperately to think of a way to get Katie Ryan into really big trouble.

*

That afternoon the triplets walked home feeling a bit confused. It was the end of the week, and they had a whole two days of doing nothing (well, apart from homework, but they still hadn't got that much of it yet) to look forward to. Somehow, they weren't feeling as good about it as they should have done. Things were definitely *not right*. Katie and Annabel still didn't want to bring up the difficult subject of Wednesday's history lesson in case Becky got upset. It meant they were having to skate round things carefully. Becky was feeling that a weekend wasn't long enough to recover from school, and wishing that her sisters weren't so good at making friends.

"So, what do you think of Manor Hill after a week, then?" Katie asked.

Annabel shrugged. "It's OK. I mean, it's school, isn't it? It could be worse. I quite like Miss Fraser, and the English teacher, I've forgotten her name. Mr Hatton's a bit scary."

Katie nodded. Their French teacher did seem very strict, and a lot of mention had been made of *tests*. "I know what you mean."

Becky listened in amazement as they chatted about the teachers, and what had happened during the week. They were so relaxed, swapping gossip about the head teacher that someone's older brother had passed on. It wasn't as though she'd hated school. The work hadn't been that hard, and although the staff seemed fairly strict, none of them had been particularly nasty. But Becky just had a miserable feeling that she didn't *fit* at Manor Hill, that she'd never be able to know what was going on like Katie and Annabel did. She'd spent most of the week sticking to her sisters as much as she possibly could, but they were both sociable, chatty things who had lots of people to talk to, Annabel especially, and Becky was really feeling like a hanger-on. She was also constantly worried that she was about to do something wrong, and it left her with a kind of heart-in-the-mouth feeling.

That evening, after tea, Becky went out to the garden shed to talk to the guinea pigs. They were very good listeners, in a furry, silent sort of way, and *they* didn't think she was stupid.

She sat on the floor in the corner of the shed stroking Vanilla, her smooth-coated white guinea pig. Vanilla's fur was very soft and strokable, and she was quite placid and happy to be held. Becky looked up at the others – Sam, Maisy and Animal – who were peering down anxiously from their hutches, worried that Vanilla was getting all the attention. "See? You don't mind being with me, do you? You like it when I play with you, even. You don't think I'm the silly one who's not worth talking to. But how come I can talk to you, but I go all silent at school? I can't even talk to Annabel and Katie at the moment." Becky grinned miserably, and swapped Vanilla for Sam. "Maybe it's 'cause you can't talk back. Probably if you could you'd tell me to shut up and stop being an idiot like Katie would."

Meanwhile, Katie was in the sitting room half watching TV and half plotting how to get Max back, and Annabel was lying on her bed in the triplets' room and painting her nails pink *and* purple because she couldn't decide which she liked best. Neither of them were concentrating properly, though, and eventually Katie wandered upstairs, and leaned on the doorframe.

"Bel. . ."

"Mmm? Which of these do you like best?" Annabel waved a hand vaguely in her sister's direction.

"Definitely purple, the pink's too sicky. Bel, do you think Becky's OK?"

Annabel considered her nails. "Maybe you're right."

"*Bel*. . ."

"All right! No, I don't think she's OK. And I

know we should try and help but I don't know what to do about it!"

Annabel sounded snappy, but Katie knew it wasn't her that Bel was cross with. It was the whole situation with Becky, and not knowing what on earth they could do.

Annabel scowled, and then dragged herself off her bed, flapping her fingers to dry the polish. "Oh, come on then. Let's go and talk to her. She's bound to be in the shed. What are we going to say?"

"Just that she shouldn't be so shy, I suppose," said Katie doubtfully.

"Hmmmm. I bet she'll love that."

"Well, you haven't got any better ideas, have you? Come on."

The two of them headed rather reluctantly for the garden, and went down the path to the smartly painted blue shed at the very end. They peered round the edge of the door. Becky was curled up in the corner, cuddling Sam, a black guinea pig with a lovely long white ruff that stuck out behind his ears. She looked up in surprise as her sisters came in. The shed was pretty much her place, and she'd wanted to be left alone.

"What's the matter?" Becky asked, feeling confused. Her sisters usually came in here only when she asked them. She felt strange, having them burst into her safe place, and suddenly it wasn't so safe any more. "Do you want me for something?"

Katie took a deep breath. "Becky – we're worried about you. It's horrible seeing you so upset. Can't we, um, help somehow?"

Becky's face was completely blank as she answered Katie, in an artificially cheerful voice. "I'm fine. Don't worry. Honestly."

Bel and Katie exchanged glances. "That's not true," Bel told her sister flatly. "You've been miserable since Wednesday, and today you've been looking as though someone's poisoned Pixie. It's because of the project thing, isn't it? Why are you upset about it?

Fran and the others seem really nice."

Becky glared back. "I don't want your help! I'm fine." She felt furiously embarrassed. It wasn't fair! She knew that Bel and Katie were just being kind, none of this was their fault, and she should let them help – but at the same time, she was so cross! How dare they? So what if they'd both got loads of friends – they couldn't leave her out and then suddenly expect everything to be OK as soon as they felt guilty for abandoning her.

"Becky. . ." Annabel sounded as though Becky was being a pain, and it was all Becky could take.

"Don't 'Becky' me! Fine, so you two are really popular – well, I'm not, and I never will be. If it makes you feel bad you'll just have to suffer – it's all your own fault for being selfish, anyway!"

Sam squeaked in outrage – Becky had been hugging him way too hard as she got more and more upset. Katie and Annabel just gaped.

They'd never seen sweet, gentle Becky get angry like this.

"Just go!" Becky hissed, cradling Sam, and stroking him apologetically.

So they went.

Chapter Eight

The rest of Friday evening was deeply uncomfortable. Mum was working to finish a translation to a tight deadline, so she missed out on the prickly atmosphere. The triplets were glad. This wasn't one of those silly squabbles about keeping their room tidy that she could jolly them out of. For once, they didn't chat when they went to bed. Katie and Annabel fell asleep quite quickly, full of righteous indignation, and Becky lay awake seething. By the time she woke up next morning, her sisters' beds were empty. Becky didn't feel like getting up. She nipped out of bed quickly and grabbed one of her battered collection of pony books. She needed comfort reading. Then she snuggled back under her warm duvet and read determinedly. Unfortunately, the ditzy heroine kept reminding her of Annabel. This wasn't working. Stupid sisters!

"Hello, Becky. You're in bed late." Mum poked her head round the door.

"Mmm," Becky replied unhelpfully, hoping that her mother's sixth sense wouldn't pick up that something was wrong. Mum could tell that things weren't right, but also that Becky *really* didn't want to talk about it, so she decided to leave things for now. She did pick up on the obvious, though. "You didn't go out with Katie and Annabel then?"

Silly question! thought Becky crossly. *She can see perfectly well I didn't!* "No, I didn't feel like it. I'm tired."

"All right, darling. I'm working this morning – just let me know if you want anything, OK?" Mum went back downstairs and Becky was left feeling aimless. She knew where Bel and Katie had gone — they'd told Mum at teatime yesterday. Bel was round at Saima's, trying on her gorgeous new outfits, and Katie was meeting up with Megan at the park to play football. Even before last night's row she hadn't felt much like joining in. Saima seemed to be so much Bel's particular friend now, as Megan was Katie's. It wasn't that she didn't get on with Saima and Megan, but she didn't like feeling that she was just tagging along with her sisters. It was so different from before — going to a new school seemed to have changed them into different people, people who didn't much like her any more.

Just then Pixie wandered into the bedroom, looking for some attention — preferably from a sensible person who would stroke her nicely while she fell asleep curled up on their bed. She turned a charm offensive on Becky to get her own way, leaping gracefully on to the bed and bounding up to her, then headbutting her lovingly on the chin, and winding her slinky body round the book. By the time Pixie's purrs had settled into sleepy breathing, Becky was feeling more determined – she had to do something. Nice though it would be to hide under the duvet all day, she couldn't stop herself *thinking*. She crept out of bed, only half-waking Pixie (who snorted in disgust and went back to sleep), and got dressed in jeans and a cosy blue fleecy top. Then she went to find Mum.

Mrs Ryan was struggling with a particularly complex passage when Becky appeared at her side. "Mmm?" she murmured.

"Is it OK if I go down to the park?"

"The park? Oh, yes, Katie's there, isn't she? Yes, sweetie, but be back for lunch, please."

Becky nodded, and headed out. She was only feeling mildly guilty – she *was* going to the park, it was just that she had no intention whatsoever of finding Katie, as Mum had assumed.

Ashfield Park was just at the end of the triplets' road, so their mum didn't mind them going there together. She wouldn't have been all that happy about Becky being there on her own, but Becky wasn't in a mood to care. She mooched down the road kicking at leaves, and peered thoughtfully through the park railings as she neared the gate. Yes, there were Katie and Megan. Becky paused as Katie took a shot at the "goal" that Megan was guarding, and grinned, impressed, as Megan pulled off a very cool save. Then she remembered that officially Megan wasn't her friend, and made briskly for the lake at the other side of the park.

It was a nice place to sit and watch the ducks. Becky wished she'd remembered to bring some bread. She sat down on a grassy bank that overlooked the water, and sighed. She needed to work out what she was going to do. If Katie and Annabel were finding new friends then she was either going to have to keep being on her own, which felt miserable, or get up the courage to make some friends by herself. She just didn't know quite how you *did* that. . .

At that moment she was practically knocked over by a big golden hurricane on legs. The gorgeous Golden Retriever woofed joyfully, and gave Becky's ear a thorough lick.

"Urrgh! You silly dog!" she told him affectionately, struggling to her feet. He was way too big to be sitting down next to – he'd nearly squashed her. "Who do you belong to, hey? Aren't you beautiful?" She petted him and he preened happily, rubbing his head against her legs. He knew quite well that he was beautiful, but he didn't mind being told.

Becky noticed that he had a lead on – just no one at the other end of it. She looked round. No one seemed to be missing this lovely boy. Still scanning the park, she picked up his lead, hoping that he wasn't really lost. The dog woofed again and set off, towing Becky behind him. She could see how he'd managed to get away from his owner – he was really strong.

He was making for a girl about Becky's age who was running towards them. Becky just had time to decide that she was almost certainly his owner before they all collided in a heap. "Sorry!" she gasped at the other girl, who'd ended up underneath.

"Not – your – fault!" panted the familiar-looking person struggling to get up. "Really – sorry! It was a – squirrel!"

Becky only looked confused for a second. Looking at the dog who'd caused all the trouble, she could see that he and a squirrel would be a *really* bad combination.

"Feathers, you are a *bad dog*!" said Fran, the dark-haired girl from school, trying hard to sound really cross. "Bad, *bad* dog!" Feathers grinned and panted happily, showing a lot of tongue. "You see!" Fran said to Becky. "He couldn't care less! He's been to obedience classes, and that's all very well for 'Sit!' and 'Stay!' – sometimes – but you don't do squirrels in obedience class! He raced off after the poor thing, and dragged me with him. I was OK until I tripped up, and even then I held on for a while and he pulled me, but then I hit a molehill."

Becky giggled.

"You can laugh, Becky – you are Becky, aren't you, it's so hard to tell you three apart – bet you've never hit a molehill at top speed."

"Sorry. You're a bit muddy, you know."

Fran looked down at her mud-smeared jumper and sighed. "My dad will kill me. You are OK, aren't you?" she suddenly asked Becky. "Feathers didn't knock you over, or anything? He doesn't mean to, he just doesn't realize how big he is."

"I'm fine – I've just got very clean ears. Feathers is a lovely name for him," Becky ventured shyly, looking at the dog's delicate – and muddy – feathery coat.

"Yeees," agreed Fran. "But don't you think it's a bit – I don't know – gentle? Sometimes I think Elephant might suit him better."

Becky laughed – much as she hated to admit

it, Katie and Annabel were right, Fran *was* really nice. She could imagine enjoying being her friend – and Feathers's. Of course, as soon as she realized this her mind went blank, and she couldn't think of anything to say. She panicked and managed to stammer out, "I'm sorry. I've got to go. Lunch. I promised Mum."

"Oh, OK," said Fran, surprised. "You're sure you don't want to—" She'd been going to say "come for a walk with me and Feathers" but Becky was already running. "See you Monday!" Fran yelled after her. "Thanks for catching him for me!"

Becky waved, and kept going.

Fran looked at Feathers, with a slightly hurt expression. "Just you and me, then."

Meanwhile, Megan and Katie had flaked out on the grass, exhausted. After they'd shared a bottle of water and recovered a bit, Megan rolled on to her front and asked, "So how do you like Manor Hill?"

"It's OK. Different though. St Anne's was really nice, but it was small, and everyone knew us – or they thought they did. We were like these identical little blonde angels, and they always called us The Triplets, not our names. This might sound funny, but I actually want to be Katie Ryan now, not just one of those cute triplets."

"I think I see – it's weird, I'd have thought it would be great having three of you. Do the other two think the same thing?"

Katie hesitated. How much private triplet-stuff should she be telling an outsider? She decided just to see how it went – it might be good to talk about all this with someone who didn't already know every detail of her life. "Yes and no. I think Annabel wants us to be together a bit less, but Becky's different. And she's having a hard time." She scowled. "We had a fight about it, last night. I don't remember ever fighting with Becky before."

"Wow. Never? I mean, don't you share a

room? How can you *never* have had a fight with her?"

"Because I fight with Bel," said Katie simply. "And Becky's the one who always sorts things out when we argue. She really hates it, you see." She grinned at Megan's confused face. "Don't worry. We'll sort it out, we always do in the end." She changed the subject. "Megan, do you know that girl in our class, Amy, with the really long peachy-coloured hair, kind of wavy? You were at Hazeldene with her, weren't you?"

"Huh!" Megan made a kind of disgusted noise. "Why do you want to know about her – she's a total pain."

"I thought she might be. She keeps looking at me and Bel and Becky in this really weird way, like we're dirt. It's not as if we've even spoken to her."

"You don't need to. She hates you, it's obvious. You're more interesting than she is. She was kind of the queen of our year at

Hazeldene – if Amy Mannering invited you round, you were an OK person to know. She was probably expecting it to be the same here, and instead everyone thinks you and your sisters are way more exciting."

Katie grimaced.

"Sorry, but you know it's true – most of us have never seen triplets before, and you *are* interesting. I bet you wouldn't like to be *totally* normal, would you?" Megan added shrewdly.

Katie smiled. "S'pose not. I'll never know, will I?"

The rest of the weekend dragged. Becky was being very silent, and Annabel and Katie kept having to stop themselves automatically talking to her. It was just natural to ask her what she thought of something, or tease her about the way she was talking to the cats. They missed her.

It was also totally obvious to their mum that something was wrong now, and to try and snap the triplets out of whatever was upsetting them, she suggested a trip to the local country park on Sunday afternoon. It was a particularly Becky-ish treat, as the park had loads of animals you could stroke, but the other two liked it as well. They agreed rather listlessly, and went to grab jackets. Mrs Ryan noticed worriedly that Katie and Annabel let Becky sit in the front of the car with no argument whatsoever and chatted in the back seat, completely ignoring Becky for the whole journey.

It was the same as soon as they got to Neale Park. Annabel and Katie disappeared immediately – their mum could see them in the distance, Annabel showing off as usual, making Katie and a whole family of little girls fall about with laughter at her impression of the meerkats – while Becky stayed close to her, stroking the tame deer. Mrs Ryan looked at her. Her hair was pulled back into two bunches, messily, and didn't look as though

98

she'd brushed it properly. She was offering one of the deer a bunch of grass, and when it turned its nose up (the entire population of the park had been offering it grass all afternoon) Becky's shoulders crumpled and she really looked as though she was about to cry.

Enough was enough. Mrs Ryan grabbed Becky's hand and marched her over to a convenient bench. "Becky, what's wrong? Have the other two said something to upset you? Please tell me, Becky."

Becky sank her chin into her jacket and refused to look up. "Nothing," she muttered gruffly. "Nothing's wrong." Sensing that she wasn't going to be able to get away with this, she added, "I just don't like school much, that's all." At least that didn't sound too babyish. Lots of people didn't like school.

"But then why aren't you talking to Annabel and Katie?" asked Mrs Ryan, confused.

"'Cause they do like it," replied Becky, just

about suppressing an "of course" which she didn't feel would go down well. "I'm just stupid, that's all." And she kicked viciously at the leg of the bench to prevent herself from starting to cry. Stupid Becky really sounded very appropriate just now – she *felt* stupid. She sniffed and stood up. "I'm going to see the donkeys, OK?" Then she walked off very fast, before her mother could start saying nice things that weren't true, so that everyone in the park saw her crying, and another whole load of people thought she was a total baby.

Over by the meerkats, Katie and Annabel were watching crossly. "I bet Mum's going to have a go at us now," said Annabel, as Becky left their mum sitting on the bench looking equally upset. But it seemed not. When Mum caught up with them she didn't mention Becky at all, just laughed at the meerkats and their cute bobbing up and down. Katie and Annabel followed her at a distance as they went on to the ostrich enclosure, and muttered to each other.

"I don't think Becky can have said we've been mean to her," mused Katie.

"But we haven't!" Annabel hissed indignantly. "It's all her!"

"I know, but Becky probably thinks we have, Bel. I wish we could sort this out somehow." Katie bit her thumbnail crossly. "I just can't work out how."

When they got back from Neale Park the triplets mooched about the house, while their mum watched them worriedly, hoping that they'd be able to sort out the problem themselves. Becky had never been unhappy at school before. Maybe she ought to arrange a meeting with her class teacher? It seemed a bit early on for something so drastic.

After staring at the television without really watching it for half an hour, Annabel surgically removed Katie from her football magazine and dragged her up to their room, leaving Becky huddled in an armchair, cuddling Orlando, who'd decided to be friendly at a useful time for once.

"We have to do something! This is so horrible! I feel like I've lost a part of myself," Annabel said, clutching her stomach dramatically.

"Stop it, Bel! You sound like you're on *EastEnders*."

"I probably will be, one day," agreed Bel. "I mean it, though. I really hate not being friends with Becky – and imagine how she feels, not talking to either of us."

"I know," said Katie, worriedly. "But what can we do? Becky's being stupid! She needs to stand up for herself at school. She basically said she didn't think we should have any other friends, and that's wrong. It's not that you and Becky aren't still my best friends, but I really like Megan. She's like – like my football friend, and Saima is your—"

"My clothes-mad friend!" giggled Bel.

"Exactly! Becky just needs a cat-and-guinea-pig-obsessed friend like her. See what I mean?"

"Of course I do, but Becky won't. Especially as we can't even talk to her! It's useless. We're going to have to try and push her into making some new mates – I've just got no idea how," Annabel said glumly.

Chapter Nine

Becky had been hoping that school might miraculously improve the second week. It didn't. She still wasn't talking to Katie and Annabel, although at least they seemed to have given up glaring at her. And now she had to deal with Mum giving her worried looks all the time as well. Mum was trying not to be obvious, but Becky kept catching her following her around with a worried little frown between her eyebrows and a bad excuse for why she was hovering halfway up the stairs.

At Monday breaktime, Fran noticed Becky sitting on the steps to one of the classrooms, reading. She wondered whether to go and talk to her, but reckoned that Becky probably wouldn't want to chat – she might disappear again, like she had on Saturday, and that would just be embarrassing. She decided to go and join in the chase game that Annabel and Katie were playing in over the other side of the playground.

Shortly before the end of break, the game broke up – everyone was shattered! Fran found herself collapsed at the bottom of the big tree with Annabel and Katie, and decided to ask them about Becky.

"Your sister's really good with animals, isn't she?"

Katie and Annabel looked at her in surprise, and one of them – Fran thought Annabel, as she had fancier hair – nodded. "How did you know? I didn't think Becky had even opened her mouth in class recently, let alone had a conversation with anybody."

"Oh, she hasn't. But I met her in the park on Saturday – she helped me catch my dog, Feathers. He'd run off after a squirrel and

Becky found him. Feathers is really big, he's a Golden Retriever, but she wasn't scared of him like some people are — so that's why I thought she must like animals," Fran finished in a rush.

Katie and Annabel felt miserable. They hadn't even known Becky had gone to the park — normally they'd have got a detailed description of any dog Becky had met, right down to the colour of his collar. It just made them feel even more determined to sort all this out.

"Did you talk to her for long?" asked Katie, thoughtfully.

"No, that's the funny thing — she ran off all of a sudden, said she had to go. I nearly went to talk to her again earlier on" — Fran nodded at Becky, still sitting reading on the steps — "but I wasn't sure if she'd want to."

Just then the bell rang, and they all headed back to the classroom. Katie smiled at Fran. "Look, don't worry. I bet she'd love to talk to you about your dog. Becky's just shy sometimes – I'm sure it'll sort itself out." *Or we'll sort it for her,* she said to herself grimly.

Becky hadn't spent her breaktime reading – she'd just been staring at her book, and mentally kicking herself for being so stupid with Fran on Saturday. There she'd been, a really nice possible-friend – with the most gorgeous dog ever – and Becky had run off like an idiot. She was going to have to apologize . . . sometime. . . She'd seen Fran hovering at break, and tried really hard to summon up the courage to wave at her. But what if Fran was cross because Becky had dashed off on Saturday? She might not want to talk to her again. Becky spent the rest of the morning moping to herself, and at lunchtime she wandered off on her own again, determined to make her sisters think she could manage without them. At the edge of the playground she nearly walked into Amy Mannering, and her two hangers-on.

"Watch it!" Amy snapped nastily, tossing her strawberry-blonde hair. Then she sniggered to her friends. "One of the little Ryan triplets – we were wrong, Cara, they're *not* tied to each other with string. Had a fight, have you?" she observed cruelly, noting Becky's woebegone face. "Your sisters decided they've got better things to do than talk to you?" Amy's friends laughed as she pointed to Katie and Annabel, both gossiping with friends.

"Leave me alone. . ." Becky quavered, looking round desperately for help. She wasn't used to being on her own in this kind of situation. The triplets had always attracted quite a lot of attention, and sometimes people were mean to them – Mum always said it was because other people found them threatening. (Becky couldn't imagine anyone finding her threatening, especially not right now.) But whenever someone decided to have a go she'd always had Katie on one side, and Katie would stand up to anyone, whatever their size. Then she'd have Annabel on the other side, making funny comments about the person who was trying to upset them. Faced with the three of them, most people slunk away after a couple of minutes, especially boys, who always seemed to get embarrassed at being laughed at by three very pretty girls who couldn't care less what was being said about them. Facing a pack of bullying girls on her own was a completely new experience, and Becky was lost.

Amy, by contrast, appeared to know exactly what she was doing. "What's it like being the boring triplet?" she taunted. "Annabel's the funny one, Katie's the clever one – what are you? Oh, I see, the crybaby," she laughed, seeing Becky's eyes fill with tears. "Go on, run and tell your big sisters we're being all mean. If you think they'll care," she added shrewdly.

Becky looked round desperately. Where were Katie and Annabel? Even though they weren't talking to her, she was sure that if they knew what was happening they'd come and help. She stared hopefully over at the group on the other side of the playground, and saw Katie and Annabel looking straight at her, apparently having some kind of argument. Annabel looked as though she was coming to help – thank goodness! – but Katie was stopping her. What was going on? As Becky watched, Annabel gave her a last worried look, shrugged and went back to the huddle, turning her back on Becky.

This had never happened before. In Becky's world, your sisters were there to protect you, always. She looked back at the sneering faces of Amy and her little groupies. What was she going to do? Tears streaming down her face, she did the only thing she could think of – she ran.

Annabel was feeling torn apart. Although she always seemed confident and had a funny answer for everything, she was also very soft-hearted, and she was gutted about what had just happened to Becky. She and Katie had been happily chatting until Annabel happened to look up, and spot Becky and her tormentors. She'd grabbed Katie's arm. "Look – isn't that Amy over there? I think she's having a go at Becky! Come on!" and she'd started to head across to sort it out, her natural reaction – no one was going to get away with something like that.

But Katie had caught hold of her sweater. "Leave it, Bel! We can't just run over there, we're leaving Becky alone, remember? That's what she wanted. She doesn't want us to help. Look, we'll talk about it at home." Katie folded her arms stubbornly and glared at Bel, as though daring her to disobey.

"But—" said Annabel, looking worriedly back and forth between her sisters, sure she could feel Becky's misery.

"*No.*" And Katie pulled Annabel round, fixing her with a stare that seemed to pin her to the ground. Katie was definitely the strongest character of the three triplets, and Annabel was just used to doing what Katie said. Helplessly, she went back to the game, casting one last worried look at Becky.

That night Katie and Annabel held a Council of War. They hadn't spoken properly to Becky since Friday evening now, and it was feeling almost painful. They still thought she was being an idiot, but just thinking that wasn't getting them anywhere. Annabel was guilt-stricken over abandoning Becky at lunchtime, and she'd convinced Katie that this couldn't go on. They were going to get Becky and Fran to be friends, whatever it took.

"I still don't see why we can't just tell Becky how nice Fran is, and what a perfect mate she'd be," argued Katie, lying on her bed and kicking her pillow crossly. They were up in their room, hiding from Mum more than Becky – Becky seemed to be spending all her time in the shed.

She'd even started doing her homework in there, generally with Vanilla curled up in her lap trying to chew her exercise books.

"Because, dimwit, one, we aren't talking to Becky, and no way is she talking to us, especially after today, and two, how would you like it if Becky and I told you we'd found a perfect friend for you and all you had to do was go and say hello? You'd kill us. No. We've got to be sneaky," mused Annabel, searching for ideas.

"S'pose so," said Katie, doubtfully.

"What kind of dog did Fran say she'd got?"

"A big Golden Retriever, why?"

"Look at that!" crowed Annabel triumphantly, pointing at Becky's chest of drawers.

"Ohhh!" Katie went over and picked up the slim photo album lying on the top. She looked at the first picture. "*Is* that a Golden Retriever?" she asked hopefully.

"Course it is, silly!" Annabel stretched out a hand for the album. "They almost all are.

Becky cuts them out of her dog magazine. You know she's desperate for a dog, and a retriever's what she'd really like. That's her dream dog."

"And Fran's *got* one. There's got to be something we can do with this!"

"Mmm. Your turn, I've had today's brainwave. Make us up a plan, Katie." Annabel flopped back on to her bed, as though spotting the photo album had taken a lot out of her.

"Well," said Katie, slowly, thinking it out. "We've got to get them both talking, haven't we? Without Becky running off in the middle like an idiot. I reckon if Fran sees this, she'll ask Becky about it, won't she? And maybe, *maybe*, if Becky's not expecting it, she'll be too surprised to be shy? What do you think?"

"It's OK, as far as it goes," said Annabel critically. "But it's not fantastic, is it? How do we get these photos in front of Fran, without Becky knowing?"

"If it was in class" – Katie paced the room as she thought out loud – "Becky couldn't run off! I think we've got to make it happen during the history lesson. Look, Becky's got a folder for all the stuff Miss Fraser's been giving us, hasn't she? And she's bound to get it out for something. We put that book in there, and there we go!"

Annabel looked at her sister. "Honestly. Is that the best you can come up with? I find you a brilliant opportunity, and that's your plan?"

Katie raised an eyebrow at her sister. She knew this game – Annabel loved being contrary whenever she could.

"Oh, all right then," Bel conceded. "Have we got history tomorrow?"

"Think so. It's a double after lunch, isn't it? We'll have to sneak the album into Becky's bag after she's got up, somehow. She'll notice if we do it now."

"Good," said Annabel in a satisfied way. "It makes me feel very *nice*, doing all this for Becky, when she's basically being a complete pain."

Katie's eyebrow went up again, and Annabel grinned shamefacedly. They both knew quite well that she was missing Becky loads, she just wasn't going to say so – not without turning it into a heartbreaking dramatic scene, anyway.

Annabel and Katie spent the next morning feeling like daring conspirators, jumping every time Becky even looked their way. By the time it got to the history lesson just after lunch, they were nervous wrecks.

"Did you put it on top of her folder?" hissed Annabel to Katie, as she passed her, on the way to sharpen a pencil that was already sharp enough to stab Max with.

"No, just underneath the photos of the school Miss Fraser gave us. Oh, I hope she takes it out soon – why am I so nervous?"

Over on her table, Becky's group were trying to work out what their project was actually going to be about. They had loads of facts – but what were they going to do with them?

"Becky," asked Jack, politely, but giving Robin a *watch out, I could be taking my life into my hands here* kind of look. "Have you got all that stuff about our school? Maybe we could do something about how it's changed?"

Becky nervously scrabbled through her folder, and Annabel and Katie gazed at each other in a kind of horrified delight.

"It's a good idea, but that's the problem – I think everyone will do that," said Fran worriedly. "It would be nice to be different – oh!" She broke off and squeaked in delight. "Becky, that looks *just* like Feathers, is that your dog? You didn't say you had one as well!" She leafed eagerly through the album.

Becky was completely confused. "I – no. That's – oh, you'll laugh. I don't even know what it's doing in here!" She looked shyly at Fran and the others. "You'll think I'm really stupid." Then she thought, *Oh, who cares, they probably do anyway.* "I haven't got a dog at all – these ones are from magazines. They're the kind of dog I'd love to have one day. You're so lucky," she told Fran enviously. "Have you seen her dog?" she asked Jack and Robin. They shook their heads. "Well, he's just like that — only gorgeouser."

"And normally muddier," grinned Fran. "You may think he's gorgeous. Wait till he's dragged you over a few molehills."

They all laughed — and Becky joined in.

"So why don't you have a dog?" asked Fran.

"Two cats," explained Becky. "And my mum says she's got enough to look after with the three of us, without a dog too. I'm working on her, though. I'm sure the cats could cope."

Katie and Annabel watched gleefully as they all chatted — it was working! Becky caught them staring, and gave a small, hesitant smile, which got her two big grins in return. She pointed Katie and Annabel out to Fran and the others. "I think those two put the album in there to make me talk to you." She gave an embarrassed grin, and looked round the three of them, even daring to catch Jack and Robin's eyes. "I'm not used to not having them to work with – sorry I've been a bit, um, weird."

"A bit? We thought you were off your head!" smirked Jack, until Fran cuffed him on the shoulder.

"Ignore him. He thinks he's funny. If you've always had your sisters around I can see it would be scary. But you're OK now?"

"Mmm." Becky nodded shyly, and smiled at Fran.

"Well, that's good, 'cause I'm not," snapped Jack. "That really hurt, I could tell Miss Fraser, you know!"

Becky turned her sweet smile on him. "Would you really? You'd tell her a *girl* hit you?" she asked, very nicely, but trembling inside that she was daring to talk back to him – this was such an Annabel thing to say. . .

Jack shuffled crossly in his seat. "Well, maybe not. I think I liked you better when you weren't talking," he added grumpily.

"Shut up, Jack, I've just had a brilliant idea," said Robin, sounding pleased with himself. "We all like animals, don't we? I've got a dog, too."

The others nodded.

"Yeah, I've got a lizard," Jack offered, forgetting to stay cross. "Why?"

"Well, why don't we do our project on animals, then?" Robin looked quite excited. "About how they've been part of our town's history. You know, carthorses, that sort of thing – there's loads of animals in these pictures. No lizards though, Jack."

"Carrier pigeons during the war," suggested Becky enthusiastically.

"Did you know they actually *ate* horses during the Second World War when there was rationing?" Jack added gleefully.

"Uurrgh!" said Fran. "That's disgusting. But interesting, too. Robin, that's a fab idea. And I bet no one else will do anything like it. Excellent!"

"Maybe we should do some research online?" Robin suggested. "I bet my mum wouldn't mind if you lot came round after school and used my laptop. 'Specially if I told her it was for homework – she might die of shock, though."

At the end of the lesson Katie and Annabel dashed up to Becky, who grinned at them. "S'pose you two think you're really clever?"

Annabel preened. "That would be because we are. It was my idea, *of* course. Katie just added a few of the finer details."

Katie rolled her eyes, and then gave Becky a hug. "Are you OK? Do you want us to kill Amy Mannering for you? We shouldn't have left you to deal with her, Becky, I'm really sorry, but I was still so cross with you."

"It's OK." Becky was feeling on top of the world – Amy didn't seem nearly as important and scary as she had yesterday. The idea that her sisters had gone to all that trouble to sort things out for her was making her feel as though she wasn't just the crybaby triplet. OK, she was the idiotically shy one, but at least Katie and Annabel cared about her enough to set up that whole stupid plan. . .

The walk home from school was very different that day. On Monday Katie and Annabel had stalked ahead, their backs radiating righteous indignation, as Becky trailed miserably behind. Today they just couldn't stop talking. It couldn't have been only four days since the row – it felt like for ever.

"Fran really is nice, isn't she, Becky?" begged Katie hopefully. "You do like her?"

"Yes, lots. And Jack and Robin too. I was so lucky to end up in a group with them. All right, Bel, you can gloat now."

"Good. We're brilliant, aren't we, Katie? Absolute geniuses, especially me." Annabel's expression was sickeningly smug, and Becky and Katie exchanged a familiar long-suffering look. It felt so good to be able to do that again.

Becky looked at them both seriously. "Sorry, you two. The whole thing was really stupid."

"You weren't being stupid," Katie reassured her.

"No," added Annabel. "She was being mind-numbingly, *unbearably* stupid. Big difference."

"Bel!" Becky and Katie looked at each other and then each took a firm grip on the jackets they were carrying – it was still too warm to wear them, but Mum insisted.

"Noo!" squeaked Annabel as her sisters launched themselves at her, flailing jackets. "It was a joke!" But by this time she was breathless after two well-aimed jackets had thumped her in the stomach, and Katie and Becky were following up with their ultimate weapon – Annabel was extremely ticklish. A couple of minutes later she was hiccuping with laughter, and begging. "Stop it! Ooh, stop it! I'll be sick! I really will!"

They all leant on someone's garden wall in a giggling heap.

"Idiot!" gasped Annabel to Becky. "You – know – I didn't – mean it!"

"Of course not," smirked Becky. "But it was a great excuse to tickle you senseless, wasn't it?"

She waggled her fingers meaningfully at Annabel's neck, and her sister squirmed back clutching her jacket as a shield. "Don't you dare!"

"OK, OK! Truce. For the moment, anyway. Listen properly now, Bel? Just for a minute."

Annabel nodded, still recovering.

"I just wanted to make sure that – that you two felt the same way I do. About us having other friends. I mean, I was really scared, 'cause I thought you didn't want us to spend time with each other any more."

"No!" Katie sounded urgent. "Becky, I can't believe you really thought that. You know we couldn't stand not being friends with you. We want to have other people around sometimes, but we're still more important to each other than anyone else."

"We're triplets, Becky – that's never going to change, ever," agreed Annabel, serious for once.

"Not even when you're being a complete muppet, like now," added Katie, pulling one of Becky's bunches in a friendly sort of way. "Isn't she, Bel?"

"Why is it that when you say something like that you don't get tickled?" moaned Annabel, pretend-cross.

Becky and Katie grinned, and pounced, and Becky explained over Annabel's wails, "Oh, because it's so much more fun to tickle you. . ."

After Robin had come up with his master-plan, Becky and Fran's project-group started steaming ahead. Becky wasn't used to working without her sisters, and she was amazed that it was actually really good. Annabel wasn't making mad suggestions all the time, and she actually got to have some say in what was going on, rather than Katie just telling her. And their project was *brilliant* – she'd seen bits of Katie's and Bel's lying around the house and she was sure they weren't as good. (Bel's was all over the stairs, her favourite homework spot. The drawings she was doing were great, as always, but her group's project was on how the school had changed over the years, and Becky was sure at least two other groups were doing the same.)

The research they'd done at Robin's (which had been really fun, going round to someone's house, and Katie and Annabel had been gratifyingly amazed that Becky was going off home with someone else) had given them loads of interesting stuff to put in. Miss Fraser seemed to think so too, and on Friday morning she dropped a bombshell.

"This is really very good," she enthused, looking at the poster-sized sheets they'd created (Becky's plan, but Fran turned out to be fantastic at art, and most of the layout was hers). "A very original idea!" Becky and Jack nudged Robin, who glowed. "I'd like you to do a presentation to the rest of the class next week – would that be all right?"

Becky froze, but Fran and Robin glared at her, and Jack poked her in the side, firmly. "Stop that! None of the rest of us want to do it either, but Miss Fraser's hardly going to let us say, 'no we don't feel like it', is she?" So Becky gulped, and just nodded determinedly.

Miss Fraser was over the other side of the room now, with Katie's group, and Max was about to pull off his plan to get back at Katie for the week before. Miss Fraser looked at their project dubiously. "Mmm. There's not really as much here as I'd expect to see. Katie, where's your work?"

"Here, Miss Fraser." Katie opened her folder to show the teacher. Only it wasn't there – the sheets she'd written up so neatly had disappeared. Completely confused, Katie turned bright red and started to stammer, making herself look very guilty.

"Hand it in on Monday, please." Miss Fraser looked very annoyed and disappointed with Katie. "Really, Katie, I hadn't expected this sort of irresponsible behaviour from you." And she swept away, leaving Katie speechless, and Max smirking like a Cheshire cat. To make matters worse, Amy had obviously heard too, and now she was whispering gleefully to Emily and Cara.

Katie rootled desperately through her bag. Could she have left her stuff at home? But no, she was sure she'd had it at the beginning of the lesson. . . Meanwhile Megan had noted the gleeful look on Max's face that Katie had been too panicked to see, and she rounded on him.

"You've taken it, haven't you? What have you done with it? You know it was there when we went to tell Miss Fraser we were ready for her to see our project – you did take it, didn't you?

You little rat!"

"Don't know what you mean," smarmed Max, his face one huge grin. "Hope you're going to do that work tonight, Katie – you're letting the rest of us down, you know."

It was obvious that Max had finally got his revenge, but Katie and Megan couldn't prove it at all – there was absolutely nothing they could do.

Chapter Ten

Katie had no choice but to redo her work for history. She did get it back – it miraculously appeared under Miss Fraser's desk at the end of the lesson – but it was ripped and covered in footprints, as though someone had jumped up and down on it. At least Miss Fraser now just thought Katie had been careless, rather than too lazy to do her homework. Katie seethed, but at least she had the old version to copy rather than having to start again. Annabel and Becky entertained her while she was copying it out by designing tortures for Max.

Becky couldn't believe how quickly the next week went – it was mostly because school was so much more fun now she not only had Annabel and Katie back, but also Fran to chat to as well, and even Jack and Robin occasionally, when they weren't being totally stupid and doing boy-stuff like trying to find out who could balance a football on one foot for longest.

It wasn't only that though. She wasn't looking forward to the history presentation, and it seemed to be getting very close very fast. The next Friday, Becky spent the whole of break going "Oh no!" and "I feel sick, honestly," and when they got to the classroom Katie, Annabel, Fran, Jack and Robin stood round her looking stern.

"Stop it!" said Katie. "You're perfectly all right and you know it."

"But everyone's going to be *looking* at me!" wailed Becky.

"Becks, it's a history project – it's not that exciting. Everyone will just be hoping that we drone on for hours so they can go to sleep with their eyes open," said Robin, rolling his eyes at the total dimness of girls.

"Yeah, or wondering whether today's cafeteria lunch is going to be disgusting or really disgusting," added Annabel.

Miss Fraser arrived then and shooed everyone into their seats. "Are you ready for your big moment, you four?" she asked encouragingly.

Fran, Jack and Robin glared at Becky, but her nerves seemed to have settled down a bit now it was actually time. "Come on, then," she said, grabbing one of their project sheets and marching out to the front of the room.

Miss Fraser clapped her hands to wake everybody up. "Right, everyone. This group have been working very hard, and they've produced a really interesting project. Over to you, Becky!"

Ten minutes later, Miss Fraser clapped very enthusiastically, and the rest of the class clapped with as much energy as they could drag up in the middle of a history lesson. The project had been quite interesting, after all, even if Amy, Emily and Cara had spent the whole time comparing their nails, and Max had whispered loudly to Ben that he'd never been so bored in his life, which got him one of Katie's best death-stares. Not that he seemed to care much.

"There, you see!" said Fran to Becky as they sat down again. "You were fine. We told you so."

"OK, but can we try not to be too good at history for a while? I really don't want to do that again in a hurry!" Becky answered, slumping back in her chair and smiling.

Mrs Ryan was feeling a bit shellshocked. The triplets seemed to have suddenly got into their new school life with a vengeance. They came home on Friday afternoon full of enthusiasm, and desperate to tell her how good Becky's history project had been, and how Becky had stood up in front of the whole class and talked. Mrs Ryan could hardly believe that these were the same girls who'd been refusing to speak to each other the weekend before last.

"So, things are going all right at Manor Hill, then?" she asked, smiling.

"Uh-huh." Three emphatic nods, and yes-type noises round mouthfuls of chocolate biscuit.

"It's fun," added Becky, managing to swallow first. "Mum, do you think we could have some friends round soon?"

Mrs Ryan positively grinned. Thinking back to how worried she'd been about Becky settling down at school, this was more than she could have possibly hoped for. "Why not? Do you want to ring them and ask them for tomorrow?"

"Yes!" Annabel actually choked on her biscuit with excitement, and leapt up to grab her mobile.

*

Next morning Becky was sitting on the garden bench stroking Pixie, who was taking a well-earned rest after catching half a pigeon (or rather, a couple of feathers from the tail-end – the rest of it had got away, leaving Pixie sitting on the grass looking disgusted and spitting feathers out of her mouth for at least five minutes, and the triplets rolling around on the grass laughing). Becky thought to herself that what she'd said to Mum was true – school was fun.

The only irritating thing was they hadn't yet managed to think of a way to get Max back for the stunt he'd pulled on Katie. But one thing was certain – Max needed to be careful, because they were *so* going to get him, eventually.

At least the six of them – the triplets and Megan, Saima and Fran – had managed the best payback ever for Amy's meanness. The best bit was, they'd nicked Amy's own idea! Every time they saw the evil threesome, the six of them would just giggle, as though they were trying desperately hard not to, but there was something so funny they just couldn't help it. It was driving Amy mad. She'd been checking her clothes, her hair, everything, to see what was making them laugh – she was obviously convinced that she had her skirt tucked in her knickers, or something. Six to three was absolutely no contest.

A couple of hours later, Orlando and Pixie were on the shed roof, sulking furiously. What had happened to their nice quiet garden? It was full of people – and a *dog*, of all things.

The dog in question was having a marvellous time. Football was most definitely his favourite game ever. Lots of people to jump up at, *and* a lovely big ball to chase.

"That dog's a better striker than you, Katie!" called Becky, as Feathers nicked the ball again, and raced down to the bottom of the garden, barking like mad.

"If only we could get him to aim at the *goal* instead of the pond, he'd be playing for Chelsea," said Fran. She was a bit damp from retrieving the ball several times already.

"Oh, look at those cats." Becky nudged her, and pointed to the shed. "They're so cross!"

"Do you think I should take Feathers home?" worried Fran.

"No way!" Annabel stroked his feathery ears. "It'll do those cats good to have Becky fussing over someone else for a bit. They think she's their personal slave."

"It's true." Becky smiled. "But that's only because I *am* their personal slave, of course. Oh, look, Mum's waving. Come on, everyone!" she called cheerfully. "Pizza!"

Even Feathers wasted no time heading for the kitchen. Delicious smells had been wafting out for the last quarter of an hour, and with six new people to look soulfully at, he was pretty sure he could manage a good feed – he was an expert, after all.

The six girls sat munching happily round the kitchen table while Feathers turned his charm on Mrs Ryan. Fran had assured her that he was allowed the occasional treat, and a few plaintive whines got him a cat biscuit in no time. He didn't seem to mind – it obviously didn't taste too different to the dog kind – but Becky thought it was probably a good thing that Orlando and Pixie hadn't seen. They might have left home.

"You see, Mum," said Becky, taking note. "He's gorgeous. And so well-behaved. We could have a dog, no problem."

Unfortunately, it was just then that Feathers effortlessly jumped up, resting his front paws on the kitchen counter, and snagged a whole packet of shortbread biscuits which he proceeded to demolish at lightning speed – packet and all.

Mrs Ryan looked down at the remains of the biscuits – just a few crumbs, which Feathers was even now hoovering up – and then up at the six shocked faces round the table. "Over my dead body. . ." she said faintly.

Everyone giggled, except Fran who looked really embarrassed. "Sorry, Mrs Ryan, he's so naughty. . ." But she cheered up when she saw that the triplets' mum was laughing too.

Becky looked sadly at Feathers. "Honestly, your timing!" she said, stroking his lovely soft ears while he grinned up at her. Still, she thought to herself, she could keep trying. And looking back to how things had been two weeks ago, she didn't think she really had a lot to complain about.

Read the opening of the
next Triplets book:

Annabel's Perfect Party

Chapter One

It was Monday lunchtime at Manor Hill School. The dining hall was full to bursting and *really* noisy. Mrs Andrews, the teacher on duty, had already had a go at shushing everybody, but now she'd more or less given up. After a weekend when they could talk as much as they wanted, and then a morning in school where they were supposed to be practically silent, lunchtime was a chance to chat – and everyone was making the most of it.

The Ryan triplets had bagged one of the choice tables in the corner by the windows. It had a good view of anything that might be going on in the rest of the dining hall, and the playground. And it was as far away from Mrs Andrews as possible. They'd had to make a dash for it right under the noses of some very snotty Year Eight girls, and there'd been some serious muttering along the lines of "How dare they?" and "Little *brats!*" But they didn't care. (Well, Becky did, but she'd just stared very hard at the kitten on her lunchbox and pretended not to hear.) Katie and Annabel had no such qualms, and gazed back at the Year Eights, Annabel with a sunny "So what?" smile, while Katie folded her arms and cheekily dared them to make her move.

"Coward!" teased Annabel cheerfully, as she banged her lunchbox down next to Becky, and flounced on to a chair. Katie gave the Year Eights one last warning glare and sat down too. "Yeah, Becky, honestly – what did you think they were going to do to us?"

Becky flushed scarlet. "It's not fair – you two are so good at arguing! I'm brilliant at it too – half an hour after whoever it is has left I've got the best comebacks. It's just that at the time I can't think of anything to say."

"Never mind," comforted Annabel. "You've got us to stick up for you."

Becky sighed. It was true, but sometimes she wished she could manage without her sisters – if she really had to.

Saima, Megan and Fran came up with their lunch trays, loaded with grim-looking school dinners.

"Excellent," said Saima happily, "I thought Marie and her lot were going to make you move."

The triplets grinned to each other as their friends set down their trays. Then Annabel made a face. "Fran, what *is* that?" she complained, pointing at the plate of something-and-chips on Fran's tray.

"Well . . . chips."

"And?"

"I don't know," Fran admitted sadly. "I was kind of dithering and the Haggis just dumped it on my plate. It *could* be shepherd's pie. That was on the menu, anyway." Everybody looked over at the counter and giggled. They could see why Fran hadn't argued. Mrs Hagan, aka the Haggis, was the head dinner lady, and she was really fierce.

"*I* know what that is," said a voice over Fran's shoulder. It was Jack, a boy from their class, on his way to the next table. "It's haggis – Mrs Hagan's speciality. You know what haggis actually is, don't you?" he added, grinning at the girls.

"No," sighed Fran, "but I have a feeling you're going to tell me. Go on."

"Weeelll . . . basically, it's bits. Bits of sheep. But the really *special* thing. . ." Jack paused, enjoying the moment. "The *best* bit, is that it's all wrapped up in a sheep's *stomach*. And that's what that is." He beamed at Fran, who looked down at her dinner in dismay.

"Ohh. Are you hungry, Jack?" she asked hopefully, as everyone groaned and made sick noises.

"No. Way." He chortled. "You're not getting rid of it that easily. Just eat the chips from round the edges, and try not to get any of the stomachy bits. . ." Then he went to sit down, still giggling.

"He is such a liar," said Becky reassuringly. "I'm sure it's shepherd's pie, Fran, honestly. Jack's just teasing, you know what he's like."

"Hmm." Fran dug her fork into whatever-it-was, and everyone watched, fascinated, as she lifted it to her mouth. And then stopped. "No. You're probably right, Becky, but I just can't. Lucky I bought a Mars bar on the way to school this morning." She wiped her fork on the edge of the plate and carefully started eating the very furthest chips.

Saima and Megan dug into their healthy salads (Saima's mum was very strict about healthy eating, and Megan took healthy eating very seriously because of football training) and the triplets opened up their lunchboxes.

"Wow!" Katie sounded gobsmacked.

"What?" Annabel asked, as everyone's ears pricked up.

"Mum's actually got our lunches right – look, she's given me peanut butter instead of your disgusting tuna like she usually does. And Becky's actually got her boring old cheese."

"Weird. I'm quite used to having to swap it all round," said Annabel through a mouthful of tuna.

"*Will* you not breathe that stuff over me! Uurgh!"

Katie reeled back from tuna fumes, fanning her face in mock disgust.

A nasty snigger floated over from the next table – someone else had obviously been listening in on their conversation. The triplets and their mates united immediately in sending a freezing glare at Amy Mannering. It was a close match between Amy and super-brat Max Carter for the person in their class that they most loved to hate. At that moment Amy was winning – she was nearer.

Amy tossed her long, wavy, strawberry-blonde hair, and the triplets rolled their eyes at each other in disgust. Amy was spoilt, stupid and seriously stuck-up – in their humble opinion. Certain that she had the entire table's attention, Amy continued her conversation with her hangers-on, Emily and Cara.

"Wasn't the girl playing Eliza brilliant? She had *such* a gorgeous voice. My singing teacher" – and here Annabel rolled her eyes again, although secretly she was very jealous, as she would have loved to have singing lessons – "says that I can start working on some of the songs from *My Fair Lady*. I'm so glad we got to see it."

"It was a great trip, Amy. You're so lucky," smarmed Emily. "And we were so close to the stage – you could see everything!"

"The restaurant was fab too," Cara chimed in. She prodded her pizza slice in disgust. "A bit different from this!"

"Oh well, of *course*," Amy said patronizingly, flicking a quick glance round to check that her audience was still with her. "My dad believes birthdays are *so* special. And as I'm an only child – well, he doesn't really have to scrimp and save, does he?" She smirked, carefully looking anywhere but at the triplets. "It's not as if there were *three* of me. . ."

"Thank God," muttered Katie, and the rest of her table burst out laughing.

"There are three of her," Becky pointed out. "Emily and Cara are just Amy without the hair."

"Forget them," advised Saima, firmly. "I'm sick

of waiting for you three to tell us. Come on, why were you all so excited this morning? What have you been looking so secretive for all day?"

Amy and co were immediately dismissed as Fran and Megan leant in to hear the news that had made the triplets giggly all through morning classes, and positively hyper at break.

The triplets exchanged glances, their dark blue eyes sparkling with mischief in an expression that made them look more identical than ever. "Weelll. . ." said Annabel slowly.

"What?" snapped Megan and Fran, together.

"It's a secret. Triplets-only. Sorryyy!" cackled Annabel, enjoying their furious faces.

"Annabel," purred Saima sweetly. "We all *know* how ticklish you are. You really, really want to stop messing about and tell us now – don't you?"

"OK! OK!" gasped Annabel, already feeling her hysterical laughter coming on. "Can we tell them?" she begged her sisters.

"I don't see why not – you're not going to be able to shut up about it for much longer anyway," sighed

Katie, and Becky nodded.

"Dad's coming home!" squeaked Annabel delightedly, "for all of half-term! Isn't that excellent?"

Saima, Megan and Fran understood perfectly just how excellent it was. The triplets didn't see their father very often as their parents were divorced and their dad worked abroad as an engineer. At the moment he was working on an irrigation project in Egypt, and the triplets hadn't seen him since early in the summer holidays.

"You'll all have to come round," volunteered Becky unexpectedly. The shyest of the triplets, she tended to leave ideas like this to her sisters. "Fran and Megan haven't met Dad yet," she pointed out, smiling at Fran. The triplets had known Saima from their old school, but they'd only got to know Megan and Fran since starting at Manor Hill that term. Fran shared Becky's complete soppiness over anything furry – especially dogs – and was the first real friend Becky'd had apart from her sisters. She was desperate for Fran to meet Dad and Dad to meet Fran. Describing her new mate in emails just wasn't the same. She was sure they'd get on.

"Definitely!" agreed Katie. "He'll really want to meet you. We can play football, Megan, he's really good, he taught me loads."

The girls beamed at each other, full of their plan. Half-term was only two weeks away – no time at all. The triplets munched their sandwiches happily, and Fran went back to poking dismally at her plate of sheepy bits.

Annabel gazed dreamily over the dining hall, planning shopping trips where Dad bought her and Saima the coolest clothes ever. Slowly chomping a mouthful of tuna and lettuce, her eyes fell on Amy and her thoughts turned to birthdays. Birthdays! Suddenly her eyes snapped wide open, she sat bolt upright and yelped. Or she would have done, except she still had the mouthful of tuna and it went down the wrong way. The yelp came out as a strangled choking noise, and she spat gobbets of tuna all over her sister, then looked at what she'd done in absolute horror (for all of two seconds).

"Bel! Oh, you are so disgusting!" hissed Katie furiously. "Uurrgh, get it *off* me! I'm going to stink of tuna all afternoon. You did that on purpose, you, you—" she became aware of Mrs Andrews's beady eyes zeroing in on their spat, and finished off in a restrained hiss, "you *thing*!"

"Shut up shut up shut up!" chattered Annabel in excitement, flapping her hands around like a mad mime artist, and only just missing Becky who was trying to pass Katie some napkins to mop herself up with. "I've just had The Most Brilliant Idea!"

Chapter Two

Infuriatingly, Annabel refused point-blank to tell anyone but her sisters about her brilliant plan. "Sorry," she told Saima, her best friend, sounding really apologetic for once. "But this really is triplets-only. I just can't. I'll tell you tomorrow, promise. Please don't be cross?" Annabel could be very charming when she wanted, gazing soulfully at Saima and looking as though a cross word would make her burst into tears.

Saima looked miffed, but gave in. She and Megan and Fran knew by now that being friendly with the triplets was great — they were all really sweet, in different ways — but it wasn't like being friends with anybody else. There would always, always be things they didn't understand, things that were "triplets-only". Still, it was worth putting up with, so she grimaced, and shrugged. "OK. But you'd better tell us tomorrow, or else. . ."

"We will. And you'll love it, honestly."

"Excuse me!" butted in Katie. "You haven't told me and Becky either, you know. When do *we* get to hear this idea, Bel?"

"When we get home," replied Annabel firmly. "I'll tell you all about it."

The rest of Monday dragged on as Mondays do. By the end of school Katie and Becky were practically putting Annabel's jacket on for her, they so wanted to get her home and talking. For once they almost wished that Fran and Saima didn't walk home with them most days (Megan lived in the other direction), and they had to try very hard not to show it. When they saw Saima into the turning for her road and they were finally alone, Katie and Becky turned on their sister with positively hungry expressions.

"OK, OK! Don't look at me like that," squeaked Annabel, quite unnerved. They were turning into their road now, and they could see Orlando, one of their two cats, prowling round the garden. He was waiting for Becky to get home and fuss over him, though he always pretended very hard that he just happened to be there at the same time every day. Becky made a kiss-kiss noise, and he gave her a very dignified "You think I'm going to come running?" sort of look before leaping (a bit clumsily, he was rather fat) on to the fence for her to stroke his ears.

"Becky!" snapped Annabel crossly. "I am about to tell you something very important! Why are you messing about with that ginger furball *now*!"

Becky picked Orlando up, and he arranged himself in his favourite position, one paw each side of her neck as though he was hugging her. It gave him the perfect opportunity to direct a pitying glare from his green marble eyes across her shoulder at Annabel – they didn't get on. Becky answered over the top of his head, "I'm not stopping you, Bel. Come on, I'm desperate for a drink. Got the key, Katie?"

Katie burrowed in her jacket pocket for the door

key. The triplets' mum was almost always in when they got home, normally doing her translation work at the kitchen table, but they liked having a key to let themselves in — it made them feel very independent.

"Mum! We're home!" Katie yelled, as she shoved the door open with her knee. The triplets' house was quite old, and though it was in no danger of falling down, bits of it did tend to stick or refuse to shut properly. It wasn't a good house for going downstairs to get a drink in the middle of the night — what with the doors and the cats, anyone would be convinced it was haunted before they were halfway.

"Uurgh! Well, I can't tell you now — we need to talk about it before we let Mum in on it." Annabel chucked her jacket at the banisters frustratedly, and didn't notice a conspiratorial look passing between her sisters — and the cat. Annabel should have told them what was going on that afternoon at school. Maybe they should pay her back. This could be fun. . .

"Annabel Ryan! I heard that! Get back there and hang your jacket up in the coat cupboard. What do you think that cupboard is for?"

"Roller skates!" yelled Annabel, rolling her eyes at the other two and scooping up her jacket again. She pulled the door of the understairs cupboard open, and it let out its usual eerie screech. Then she leaned riskily across three pairs of in-line skates, a large bag of woodchip for Becky's guinea pigs and a skateboard, to reach the hooks at the back of the cupboard. "You'd better pass me yours as well while I'm here," she said in a coat-muffled voice. "Ow!"

"What?" asked Katie worriedly, poking her fleece round the door. "Are you OK, Bel?"

"Yeah, I just stabbed myself on that stupid cat-carrier again. Those spiky bits on the door are dangerous."

"Sorry," called Becky, attempting a complicated one-armed jacket-removing manoeuvre without putting down Orlando, who was acting superglued because he knew it would make life difficult. "I think Mum's having one of her tidiness-fits again," she added in a lower voice. "She doesn't normally mind if we put stuff on the banisters."

"It probably all fell on her," came the muffled voice again, accompanied by an impatient hand. "Come *on*, Becky – jacket!"

Katie tugged Becky out of the sleeve she was struggling with and passed the jacket over. Annabel emerged dustily from the cupboard looking like she'd been on a dangerous mission.

"Right," she whispered. "Get juice and biscuits and then we're going to our room. I'm going to be sick if I don't tell you this idea soon."

"Serves you right," Katie whispered back, grinning. "You shouldn't have been so secretive at lunchtime." Then she led the way into the kitchen where their mum was working at the big pine table. Mrs Ryan translated books from German or French to English, and the other way round. This meant she could do most of her work at home, which made being a mum easier too.

Mum smiled up at the three of them. "Hello!

Did you have a good day? Sorry, I've got to finish this bit off, and then we can do tea. Grab yourselves a snack for the minute."

The triplets looked around the kitchen. Yes, apart from the table, which had lots of books piled up on it and several abandoned cups of coffee, the kitchen was looking unusually tidy. Positively shiny, in fact. They sighed. They wouldn't be able to find anything while Mum had this fit on. At least it wasn't likely to last very long. Annabel looked at her mum, who'd just got up to put the kettle on, while Katie grabbed apple juice, and Becky, still one-armed due to Orlando, rootled for biscuits. Mum looked stressed, Annabel thought. Probably too much tidying – the kitchen was hardly recognizable from this morning, and now she came to think of it, the hall had been scarily neat as well.

"Let's go and get changed. OK, Mum? We'll be down in a bit, to help with tea, all right?" And she exchanged meaningful looks with Katie and Becky.

Mum obviously wanted to get back to work – Annabel could tell from the way she kept casting jittery looks at the table – and she didn't complain. "OK, you three. I should have this done in another half an hour, I think."

Annabel shooed her sisters upstairs as fast as she could. They paused worriedly at their bedroom door – no, it was OK, Mum's tidiness mission hadn't got this far, *yet*. Katie gave Becky another conspiratorial look behind Annabel's back, and wandered over to the chair by her bed and started burrowing through the pile of clothes on it.

"What are you doing?" shrieked Annabel, who was jumping up and down with impatience by now.

"Finding some clothes to change into," answered Katie, puzzled. "You said—"

"I didn't mean it! Sit down!" gibbered Annabel. "You two are doing this on purpose, aren't you?"

Becky smirked. "Might be. Might not. . . Oh, come on, Bel, you know you can't keep secrets, 'specially not from us. You shouldn't have tried to make us wait for so long. Maybe we don't *want* to know, now. . ." Then she caught the frustrated, hurt look on her sister's face and melted. "Oh Bel, I'm sorry. We do want to know, don't we, Katie? Look, I'll even put Orlando out of the room, so you can see I'm really listening." She slipped the cat out of the door and closed it before he'd had time to work out what was going on.

Annabel smiled gratefully. "I wasn't trying to make you wait – well, only a little bit. It's a really good idea, honestly."

Katie and Becky sat down on Katie's bed and gazed up at Annabel, the picture of attention. Annabel took a deep breath, beamed at them and started. "I suddenly thought of it at lunchtime, when those idiots were droning on about Amy's brilliant birthday party. Do you remember what Mum said in July when we were eleven?" (The triplets' birthday was July 4th. American Independence Day – Mrs Ryan always said it had obviously had a real effect on Katie.)

"Oohhh!" breathed Becky and Katie together, starting to realize what Annabel was getting at.

"You see? She said we could have a party if we wanted but then Dad couldn't be there in the summer, except for that one week he was taking us to Wales, so she said why didn't we wait until we'd started at Manor Hill and Dad got some holiday and then we could have Dad at our party and lots of new friends and—"

Her sisters were looking at her goggle-eyed. "Bel, breathe!" snapped Katie. "Honestly, that's the longest sentence I've *ever* heard anybody say in one breath. You're crazy."

"I can see why though," nodded Becky. "It's a great idea, Bel. You're so clever!"

Annabel subsided on to the bed next to them, looking oxygen-starved but happy. She raised her eyebrows hopefully at Katie. Being the oldest of the triplets (by two minutes; Becky was the youngest, a full half-an-hour younger than Annabel) she tended to make most of the decisions – until the other two argued her out of them, anyway.

Katie grinned at her sisters. "It's excellent, Bel.

Well done for remembering, I'd forgotten about it completely." She carefully banished the nasty, niggling little voice that was wishing she'd thought of it first, and bounced up from the bed. "Come on! Let's go and tell Mum!"

Look out for more
Triplets

HOLLY WEBB

Triplets

Annabel's Perfect Party

HOLLY WEBB

Triplets

Katie's Big Match

HOLLY WEBB

Triplets

Becky's Problem Pet

HOLLY WEBB

Triplets

Annabel's Starring Role

HOLLY WEBB

Triplets

Katie's Secret Admirer

HOLLY WEBB

Triplets

Becky's Dress Disaster

Look out for

Look out for

HOLLY WEBB

EMILY FEATHER
and the Enchanted Door

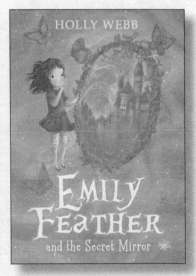

HOLLY WEBB

EMILY FEATHER
and the Secret Mirror

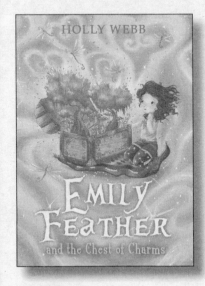

HOLLY WEBB

EMILY FEATHER
and the Chest of Charms

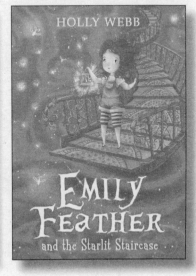

HOLLY WEBB

EMILY FEATHER
and the Starlit Staircase

HOLLY has always loved animals.
As a child, she had two dogs, a cat, and at
one point, nine gerbils (an accident).
Holly's other love is books. Holly now lives
in Reading with her husband, three sons
and a very spoilt cat.

TEN QUICK QUESTIONS FOR HOLLY WEBB

1. Kittens or puppies? Kittens

2. Chocolate or Sweets? Chocolate

3. Salad or chips? Chips

4. Favourite websites? Youtube, Lolcats

5. Text or call? Call

6. Favourite lesson at school? Ancient Greek (you did ask. . .)

7. Worst lesson at school? Physics

8. Favourite colour? Green

9. Favourite film? The Sound of Music

10. City or countryside? Countryside, but with fast trains to the city!